First Printing 2021

Book and cover design by 3hats.com, Seattle, WA

ISBN: 978-1-7351791-4-8 print version
ISBN: 978-1-7351791-5-5 epub version

Published by Roger Road Publishing
3661 East Roger Road, Tucson, AZ 85718

ROGER ROAD
PUBLISHING

Celestial Rhythm

Book Three:
Memoirs of a
Road Warrior

Steven Polinger

The old ways were gone! Politics and religion had given way to the practice of honesty in all interactions. Not so, in the bad old days.

Like politics, religion was a construct of man. Subject to fabrications. For example, that faith alone, without living it in just action, had any wings at all. Instead, to enter relationships not made by human hands. No spiritual infection could contaminate the ones that have a true heart.

They were the rainbow bridge, of return and revival. On the wings of vast spiritual cleansing. To inspire the Sacred Hand to guide us. The new way.

The deception that evolution and creation are in conflict sets up antagonism between believers and scientists. The actual reality is that creation and evolution are part of the whole unity of life itself. They are one. Evolution is the continuance of creation.

Reality cries out to us to redefine evolution and creation as a single, greater, force of life.

Chapter One
The Absolute Nature of Reality

In the year 2031 AD, Eleazar spoke with force, as his eyes danced with intensity. As usual he had an axe to grind with stupidity. Everybody loved seeing this gentlest of souls get fired up with feeling—as a scientist and man of faith.

"Deception provides a twisted view of reality. It is the primary tactic of war. Like the lie that evolution and creation are in conflict. Satan loves this one. It sets up conflict between believers and scientists. To kill truth. The actual reality is that creation and evolution are part of the whole unity of life itself. They are one. Because evolution is the continuance of creation. Joined together by life. To sustain life by creating through evolution.

"The first breath of life was meant to give life to the ends of time, for all that evolve. These two, are vital, in unity, for all life. It is preposterous to suggest otherwise! The breath that God breathes into Adam, is the Ruach Ha Kodesh or Sacred Wind, also called the Holy Spirit. The breath of life is spirit. For all that lives.

"Reality cries out to us to redefine evolution and creation as a single, greater, force of life. The creative process of evolution. Environmental stress triggers adaptation in the process of natural selection. The imperative is for life to go on. Life is the primary, elemental force. Rewritten genetic code provides survivability. This is the opposite of random! It is the code that is writing life.

"Existence is not a random event, the dynamic to cause it must occur. The causal force is God. His purpose is an entire vision. From the vision comes intelligent life. In a conversation giving birth to the evolution of the spirit. This animating force, springs forth, from His intention, His plan. Choose between randomness or purpose. Either everything means nothing or else everything means something."

Then Walter spoke, "Satan knows how to start a quarrel. Like the argument that we must choose between creation or evolution. This cunning trickery is how he kills. Like using fear, to get us motivated for vaccinations. Vaccines that retard our immune response, to a moving target. Overturning our naturally developing, immune response, to constantly mutating, viral strains. As these strains grow more deadly, and our immune systems weaken, by forming immunities to an ever mutating, virus, we miss the actual target, thus selecting out hardier quasi-species, leaving greater casualties. Also, having our selves injected, with the chains of slavery. For in those vaccines are nanoparticles and micro-biochips. To enable their cashless beast system. Without this mark, they will be unable to buy or sell."

Jake smiled during gunplay. The deadly arts were pleasurable. He used to say, "Don't forget to smile during a gunfight. It's what we do, whether or not we are playing for keeps." He would interrupt Walter with his daydreams, and Walter was used to his occasional unruliness.

Walter then continued, "Shifting gears, the Angels that warned Abraham about the destruction of Sodom and Gamora, were asked by Abraham, 'will you stay your hand for those righteous there?' They answered, 'Ye but then only Lot and his daughters could be rescued. The Great Tribulation has been unleashed, to literally rescue the righteous. Without this cleansing storm, no righteous could be rescued. The rampage of Covid19-strains are biblical plagues."

To search and find in full dimensionality, what is real, the actual is. With regard to anything we wish to experience. Real discovery sends energy to all the other related information. Dreams waken us to the deeper meanings. As souls evolve, dynamically new insight, supports the expanding vision. In this new paradigm, all living beings continue evolving. A function of …how it is! To experience reality is euphoric.

Ari said, "Our living process with our Maker, is instilling continual life. We are reborn every instant with renewed life. Not even terrible injury or grave illness can stop this flow of love, carrying us from strength to strength. We are carried by Divine arms, the whole Kingdom of Heaven."

Hebrew for prayer. Yiddish for laughter. Ari means lion. Lev means heart. Lion Heart! Earth had only a thirty-five-year tribulation. Everywhere else had a thousand-year tribulation. Many Earthers experienced both. They joined the struggle to cut Satan down!

Jake's Rabbi, Ari Lev, Lion Heart, "The endless expanse has within its core, the endless expanse of telepathic web conversation. The total Unity, of Life Giver and all living beings, brings the illumination of reality. The euphoric elixir. The cup of this brings delight to all of us as one.

"Our web conversation, sometimes wordlessly, brings the truth of actual reality. Revelation gives birth to this dynamic revolution of vision. These transmissions have transformed us, we can hear Life Giver and all other voices. We have evolved to the point that our realizations have expanded us, just as the endless expanse of space.

"We expand in this mirror of light, bringing us into the infinite of experience. Awareness without end. We merge with Life Giver while we remain in our physical bodies, to drink from the cup of eternity."

Lion Heart was a noble singer. When the resurrected began flying for the Alliance, he was the first to sign up among the holy warriors. History classes could now use time travel to closely observe the actual events as they took place. All species could thus observe what truly happened on any home world they wished to study. So many history books were to be discovered as based on lies that warped the telling of each specie's story. Religions found greater depth, for example, in being with the prophets, in their discoveries. So many religious books and history books were rewritten with marvelous insights into myriad lives.

A student of American black history could visit the greatness of Hannibal, King of Carthage, an illustrious example of the black king who nearly rescued the world from Roman oppression. An astounding experience of powerful military leadership, that nearly freed the world from slavery to Rome.

For another example, on Earth, the battle to cleanse the churches, mosques and synagogues of their rampant twisted corruption. The efforts to drive a stake through the heart of those manipulations of Satan. To remove the quest for wealth and power from within the bloated, big business, religious cartels, that drove God from their midst. This cleansing then opened them toward a return to Life Giver. Releasing the iron grip of the seductive lies that strangle. To open a clear view into what actually is. To hear the song of life.

How the Source of all Life chose individuals to go to each defiled organization, to call out their atrocities. In partnership, this calling out by Divine Law, was required, before a contingent of Angels were sent to prosecute the greater battle. To cleanse or condemn each faltering organization, more harmful and farther away from God than the secular realm. Life Giver waits for willing partners, to open Heavens Gates in response. Armies of Angels, called to action, by the voice of a man.

In ancient Israel, God was King, until Saul took over, for those who clamored for a 'real king.' Then came David, after Saul failed to follow the sound council of God, through His Prophet Samuel.

David showed his people how a King might rule while governed by God, demonstrating that liberty is the Law of God for those that walk with Him, providing every good thing as result.

Early Americans desired to walk with God. Divine interventions kept America's fight for Independence on its feet, to escape tyranny. On the wings of miracles, our liberty prevailed. God's will is done, when a free country finds its course, following the way of God.

Into our hearts, He sent His laws and His ways, for us to govern by. From God, laws derive their authority.

Chapter Two
The Cradle of life

The name Yael means the Lord is God, Kohane is the lineage of Priesthood. Yael Kohane, and Ruarie MacNeil, were pals. They lived on the home world of Nomiru. They were feisty young women, who had fought, as singers, during some of the last, truly hairy battles. They had been swimming in a blue lake and were now ready for conversation.

They went back in time, to the nineteen sixties, to a wonderful Mexican village, to witness a brutal firefight, in order to dress the wounds of a man who would one day lead his people into the light of freedom, making Mexico, eventually, a very great nation. Pablo Reyes was an elegant soul.

"As a Catholic, it is clear, that when we are wearing His huaraches, we are walking His path. Walking in His footsteps."

Then they bounced to encounter, in another dimension, themselves as they would be, had they been born another time and place. They were sitting by another lake and in another place-time.

Ruarie, "My blood burns like fire. The people have no comprehension of the nature of evil. When will they ever learn? Only in tribulation! When their civilization lies shattered at their feet?"

Yael, "Their will to render good, impotent. Their orgy in self obsession has created the vacuum, where once our Creator stood by us and has become the haunt of demons. They embrace evil unknowingly, when they turn away from the only source of good. The nature of evil is to destroy, to expand within great nations, until they die."

Ruarie, "I'm telling it from my heart. I don't lie to myself! Revelation is revolution, to know history is to understand both present and future. Like in black history, on June nineteenth, 1863, the day of emancipation, for all slaves. What if they knew their own history, not just the culture and language of their origins, but of the great ones that came before them. Juneteenth was a game changer, but how about this, Hannibal! His Carthaginian Empire, in North Africa. Perhaps the greatest military genius of all time. Who nearly ended, the Roman Empire, that made slaves of all who they conquered, as they continuously gained territory. Hannibal was one of the greatest kings who ever lived."

Yael, "Teach the people their history, to empower them, with God life and freedom, for their foundation."

Ruarie, "There is also very little comprehension of good, although it is romper room simple. Our Creator is a freedom lover, among His many gifts to us is freedom. Satan is a freedom snatcher, ensnaring with poison, from his hatred of freedom."

Yael, "In conversation, speak the word freedom and see who lights up and who goes dark. Freedom is the law of God. As simple as traffic lights, you will see who leads them. For reference, a good example can be made comparing Churchill and Hitler. Some will go either light or dark, luminously, for one or the other.

"Those that choose against the light of freedom, will be eaten alive by demons. Wandering blind, into the jaws of death. Those alight and aligned with freedom, find Divine Favor. So it is that revelation gives birth to this dynamic revolution of vision."

After this, the feisty two bounced back to Nomiru. More Humans lived on Nomiru than on Earth. There were many more Humans living in other worlds than Earth. The two had bounced back to their blue lake. All the transmissions, from all the experiences, could be picked up by all Living Beings. They could be stored for posterity, referenced by who what where and how. Kept as volumes, in the great treasure house of consciousness.

"Study history to find out where you are going. A history of consciousness to be included. How do you find your path? Go to that place of the beginning, within your soul. The first steps in the evolution of your soul. Your soul had direction, found by your very nature, that came from the Hand of the Life Giver." This teacher was tough. His historical perspective was that all truth came from one source.

"Every soul eventually joins the fray, in their search for the truth and the meaning of their life. Every battle plan seems perfect just before the crossing of swords. Every battle needs a miracle. While we resolutely hold the line, never to count the cost. Having that deliberate intention to break the strength of the Adversaries devises and deception.

"We look ever upward, to our Source. We circle clockwise as do both our souls and planetary orbits. We open ourselves into seeing, in the black darkness, where it is clear that the soul can see from within our bodies. More deeply than the eye." Another teacher from within the circle began to speak.

"With a speed that is out of this world, the question arose, what if we went back in every timeline, to throw a bolt of lightning through every false leader, teacher or preacher, so the light could pass through them? The derisive laughter of demons hissed back the answer. 'We will just plug the holes and our legions are everywhere at once. Don't you know that Satan is loosed to harm as much as possible in his time remaining.' This testing builds our strength of will, to see it through.

"This long journey has the purpose of cultivating souls in their evolution. We have legions also. All creation will one day walk together as one into the eternity, of our lives. These lessons impart understanding as to our very nature. The end of the dark struggle will be our leaping forth, place, in our elevated and accelerated evolution. The endless dark, pierced by the light of creation and vanished before the face of its splendor."

History classes had changed a lot. This the result of the evolution of the soul. Conversations now could be had through any time, place or dimension, so travelers could ask for guidance from anyone, anytime. Because of the great increase in spiritual intelligence, young children, even toddlers, could "bounce" or flow, dimensionally. But back to history.

Teacher, "War takes a warrior, to places no one can follow. To oppose evil sets a warrior on a path of direct conflict with the forces of evil. Human history is filled with governmental injustice.

"In ancient Israel, God was King, until Saul took over, for those who clamored for a 'real king.' Then came David, after Saul failed to follow the sound council of God, through His Prophet Samuel. David showed his people how a King might rule, while governed by God. Demonstrating that Liberty is the Law of God, for those that walk with Him. Providing every good thing, as result.

"Early Americans desired to walk with God. Divine interventions kept America's fight for Independence on its feet, to escape tyranny. On the wings of miracles, our liberty prevailed. God's will, is done, when a free country finds its course, following the way of God.

"Any study, of the war, makes it clear, that we enjoyed God's favor throughout. Into our hearts, He sent His laws and His way, for us to govern by. Giving us the chance to govern ourselves in freedom. To be responsible to see that justice is done. Biblical law informed the founders, in their writing of the Bill of Rights and Constitution."

Student, "To conquer a free people, only takes confiscatory taxation. Introduced progressively, they will never know what hit them. A democratic republic runs by the peoples will. An empire runs by control. Circa 2020AD on Earth, California, for example, or the EU, or Russia, or China."

Student, "Subdue the people's freedom, by forcing them to comply with unending bureaucratic control. Then close the borders so that no one can escape. Put a chip in their hand or forehead, to monitor them and keep them from their own resources, through a cashless nightmare. California had a steep 'leave the state' tax for those brassy enough to think they are free. As long as you have anything, they can take it."

Time travel to anywhere is commonplace. Discovering to a greater intimacy and depth, actual history as it happened, with a much closer look into whatever aspect Bouncers wanted. Anyone could be anywhere. Naomi, speaking through time, to the Earthers enveloped in chaos. "Are we a terminal species to be called 'endling?'" Many of the voices that some were able to hear, were actually higher beings speaking through time, to the higher soul roots of those, that were ready to expand their evolution.

"Our Father speaks to you through all his messengers. So that you have always been given the choice to be endlings or not." Then, speaking into the present, "Now that we can just call it and go, without any apparatus needed, we can send ourselves to dimensions, times, places and even combined dimensions, to experience, learning each day can be explosively edifying. Although we are under the direct command of Life Giver, His sovereign wish is to empower us and aid us in our quest for discovery. To let us go out and play, to teach ourselves, in concert with all other living beings, we are making our own future.

"There may be dimensions or places, where things are not going well. Here we partner discoveries to heal the broken worlds left behind in the wake of the great rampage of Satan. Our responsibilities are to heal the vast populations suffering under the profound levels of post traumatic stress. Like the home world of Xzanphoria, where Xzanphors were kept as slaves, in unspeakable cruelty and torture. For tens of thousands of years. Loving interaction is the way forward, to bring them out of inner conflict. On billions of planets, trillions of victims urgently need our help."

Say no to the hellish hordes of temptation. No to the personality cults, no to the vast retail religious organizations, that mine for gold instead of teaching the way of the heart of gold.

Retail religion and politics have nothing to do with God at all. Our churches are scandalously self-seeking instead of doing real service. All that drives people away. It is the fruit of this evil manipulation, to destroy the churches from within.

A great return, a great revival, depends on our true heart. Standing up and taking action. Our goal is to bring God back into these stumbling organizations.

Chapter Three
Hard Work

The time was November ninth, 2014, seven days before Earths Great Tribulation. Amazingly, few seemed to know. A deepening sense of foreboding lingered everywhere. America had lost track of their own identity, in the land of the free. Small and unimportant things filled the minds of most everyone.

Unity was being traded off for howling polarization. The fight was on, over nothing that mattered. Wrathful, raging masses of anger blinded victims, leading them to incessant conflict. The hidden force behind the hidden agenda: that of an insurgency for Marxist insurrection. So well disguised, by a covering of anarchist chaos.

The fight was on, so that few could discern, the march toward a civil war, facing the once great republic. How could something so obvious, be so undisclosed. That is the very way that satanic manipulations work, by total stealth, clouding the minds of all his victims. The way Hitler hoodwinked the world, long enough that he got away with it. Yes, it was happening again, in the plain view of the fearful confusion, the hook to get it through. The global hypnosis was gradually gaining steam. To lie only a little bit of the time.

Those times of greatest stress and testing are also the wellsprings of the Sacred Wind, riding on the sails of eternity. In a tiny church, out of the way, an impassioned pastor spoke. "God is wellspring to life. We walk with God to find sanctified purpose. A warrior makes a plan. Otherwise defeat is imminent. From God, laws derive their authority. Truth and freedom are sustained by God's laws. Most importantly, God is One! The Jews say, 'Adonai hu Ha Elohim.' Which means, The Lord is Creator. The Muslim say, 'Allahu Ha Achbar,' which means, the Most High is Almighty. We say, 'God is: Father, Son, Holy Spirit.' In all these, God is One!

"Say no to the hellish hordes of temptation. No to the personality cults, no to the vast retail religious organizations, that mine for gold instead of teaching the way, of the heart of gold. This heart of gold, acts justly, loves mercy and walks humbly. This true heart has no need to campaign for more money and influence, turning the faithful into checkbook, credit card Christians, with no time to sacrifice, toward serving others in need. But the true heart is always instructive and inspiring.

"Retail religion and politics have nothing to do with God at all. Our churches are scandalously self, seeking instead of doing real service. All that drives people away, is the fruit of this evil manipulation. To destroy the churches from within. A great return, a great revival, depends on our true heart. Standing up and taking action. Our goal is to bring God back into these stumbling organizations."

Back in 2013, the senator from Louisiana, Tom Horn, was speaking to a gathering of his closest friends and allies. He had become a young statesman. He would become a consequential leader. He believed the Great Tribulation would be a global exorcism.

"America is under siege. To keep freedom requires the sacrifice of service on the part of those who are blessed to be living in freedom. To defend it from those aggressors who seek to destroy it. The Marxist globalists are against our freedom. They are out to take a prey from without, but more alarming, from within. We need to push back in a concerted effort, or they will roll right over us. Half the nation welcomes this freedom snatching from within. That is the real peril of our time. Always one election away from slavery. We Americans are dancing on our own graves.

"The chosen will be called to speak out and accuse all the practitioners of false religion and political darkness. They infest our churches, synagogues and mosques, our schools and news media. They are the dark underbelly of our current state of hidden insurrection. They have grown their malignancy, into our much compromised, election system. Democracy is their target. A nasty form of global Marxism awaits with open jaws, to eat what is left of our freedom. Yet we have become our own worst enemy. Our own disunity is the engine of despair.

"Together, we must find the way, to revive ourselves and take the fight to the enemies of freedom. To regain our independence and quell the coming revolution and civil war. Together we will return, to all that has made us free and creative. Until we return to the Almighty, as the center of all we do, we will continue to flounder. We are being invaded from within and without. By the grace of God, we can win back all His blessings, the very foundations of freedom. We will win if we stand up. Either that or we fall.

"So, we take back America from her current demise. Lifting up Lady Liberty from among the jackals, who have occupied, to overthrow. Now or never, we have run out of time to act, because we all see the battle lines drawn. Now we stand in the place of our founders, to keep what they gave us."

Then suddenly they began to pray. The statesman brings honor, wherever he may go. He lights the path for all to move together. A politician has only his own honor. A statesman has God's honor, like Washington or Jefferson. Their lives are historically relevant.

A person grows with the greatness of his task, moving the evolution of his soul. Moving close to eternity, it had come time, to stand up and send a spear, through the vitals of church corruption, at the higher levels where demons feed.

Only through Divine proximity, was it likely, that they might even scratch the surface. But the call came. It was urgent and intense. They who heard the call, did not know where to begin. They would wait in prayer, feeling overwhelmed. But they knew, there would be a plan, and a series of steps to be taken. Humbly, they felt, who were they, to be given this? They were to name and identify the wrongful. That alone, would set loose, the powers beyond, to do battle.

During the Great Tribulation, the foundations of all of mans constructs, would be shaken in the fierce winds of total change. Most of all, the church. For the cleansing that makes sacred or the absolute death. Without the pressure of tribulation, the cleansing could not be done. The addicted were fiercely opposed and many would die. They had never been part of God's Kingdom and oppressed those who were. But once called out by their deeds, they were answered by the consuming storm of the Great Tribulation, followed by the Great Blessing, to remake everything. For the cleansing that leads to accelerated evolution.

Whenever we look into the future, that alone changes it!

The beginning of political religion came with Adam and Eve. God supplanted by government. They would decide for themselves about good and evil, without God's guidance. Since they had expelled God, they would be expelled from Eden. So, they could invent, whatever civilization or government they wanted. According to their will. Turning away from Life Giver and toward themselves as the ultimate guiding light. Away from the Light of Creation, to the fog of nation, the path of shattering rage and defiance began here.

The politics of Covid19, was how they would martial in the Beast System. Either God rules, or else Satan will.

Our souls lead us to discovery, in union with Creator, to see our own true path. Not always consciously, but now, our destiny becomes the reflection of our soul's guidance.

Chapter Four
The Steepening Curve

Digital Totalitarianism, with injected nanoparticles and micro-biochips, were used by big tech, big bank and big news media, to have it their way politically. Watching the many ways elections were manipulated, gave the spiritually sensitive, poison headaches and the shivers.

Many heard the shrieks and howls of demonic derision, like victory cries and counting coup. With darkness blowing out all the candles and strangling freedom. The Global Oligarch's plan was to defy both God and death and rule with an absolute iron hand. Big tech, big media, and big pharma, fired the furnace of wrath, hastening the storm of judgement and the winds of tribulation.

Those who would not be contaminated would find their way to stay alive and open the path to accelerated evolution. At the end, at the Return of the King. To drink from the cup of eternity, sitting at the banquet table of everlasting light. They stand as one before all. Having held the line.

Shifting focus to another place in time. He had wrestled with evil, learning that he must oppose it. God alone was infinite, is infinite and will be infinite. He has been "verbing" all His creation, from His infinite "is."

"We cannot truly live, without something we would die for. Lovers of freedom know. The others are too afraid, lazy or clueless." Jake mused, "Nobility does not come by birth, but rather by our actions."

Having near death experiences gave him practice facing death in peace. He would not want to ruin a warrior's death by feeling any fear, but rather walk into whatever is next with a happy and open heart. If God is with us, then what is there to fear. He would go on thanking his Maker as he looked forward to seeing His face.

Jake fell desperately ill again. He went to his surgeon's office and just as he entered, pus burst out suddenly, shooting all around the office. Dancing a highland fling with his right hand lifted, he sang, "I am a cavalier, in the shadow of death, I have no fear!"

Though he started as a pitiable waif, he would end in magnificence. He was without fear, as the puss blew out of him like a volcano. During surgery he received great blessing and deliverance. When he awoke, he felt a euphoric joy. He could clearly see what had just happened on the operating table. The room was full of a misty gleam of softest purple. Angels standing guard over him, keeping him alive. Lots of metal, rotted flesh and brown puss was taken away from his life, so he could live. "Thank-You, Father, for always catching me before I fall." "You would not fall My son, you will rise."

It was the fall of 2020 and Jake was so thankful, even though America and the whole world were really going crazy. Cash had been banished from Sweden to India and many other nations. Cashless meant control. The world wanted control of the citizenry. The writing was on the wall, cash allowed a little freedom and freedom was the enemy!

To release fear, the faithful simply move beyond it and the paralysis it invokes. Few warriors are without transcendent faith, because fear kills. With God there is no fear but letting go and opening up. To be filled with the mystery of Life Giver's boundless love. The uncontainable and creative gift, the wonder of God's Grace.

Trust of God had filled Doctor Tom's hands, guided by his Maker. The power of this presence, beyond words. Jake knew that miracles had taken place. His ability to reach out to others was enhanced. Instead of feeling sick for a year after, like the last time, he felt great. Tom said, "Another miracle has taken place, or you would not feel so great. Your life bares testimony, to witness what you can share. The last time you lost a hundred pounds as you spent a year next to death.

"This time, you are ready to go sailing. You believe in miracles and so they are just normal for you. This is a teachable moment, to help you reach out to others. Tell your stories to open hearts and lead them. Your walking in miracles is the telling of great deliverance, go tell it on the mountain. The mountain of deliverance." Then, a few months later, they rebuilt his neck.

Again, the afterglow of the Presence followed him. Radiant tranquility touched him with loving hands. Words cannot paint this picture. He realized that Angels had always been there, and whatever the tribulation, they always would be. Transcending fear with trust calls them, by God's Grace. Just as Doctor Tom was his brother, so were the Angels, his sisters and brothers.
Another shift.

Looking for trouble is a great way to find some and pick a fight. Where there was no justice, warriors made some. Thus obviating, that even the evil ones must bow before God's might, when warriors were called to co-create justice in those places that were without. Warriors were more about prayer and not just physical combat. God loves justice and those who take action on behalf of justice, including healers and providers of food for the hungry. Life is more powerful than death. Places without justice, lead to enslavement and death.

Naomi was again speaking through time. "The action of calling out to God for justice, enlivens all creation to the highest Angels, to respond with action. Prayer refines and cultivates us. We have discovered what the evolution of a soul looks like. The journey is leading toward the dynamic of experiencing how we are made in Life Giver's image. Looking up toward Creator, our souls open. Looking out, our souls revolve, in confluence with planetary orbit. The Light of Creation illuminates our souls and when we have evolved enough, we can help others to find their own direction.

"Our souls lead us to discovery, in union with Creator, to see our own true path. Not always consciously, but now, our destiny becomes the reflection of our soul's guidance.

"Savage division, and fierce hatred, is a product of disconnection and unparalleled evil. All the rage of all the defiant tyrannizers, comes from the guilt and thus hatred towards their victims and slaves. Cleaning up on aisle three, happy shoppers.

"The beginning of political religion came with Adam and Eve. God supplanted by government. They would decide for themselves about good and evil, without God's guidance. Since they had expelled God, they would be expelled from Eden. So, they could invent, whatever civilization or government they wanted. According to their will. Turning away from Life Giver and toward themselves as the ultimate guiding light. Away from the Light of Creation, to the fog of nation, the path of shattering rage and defiance began here."

Emperor Constantine circa 325 AD, was the human architect of diabolical planning. To go after the faithful and seize power from God. Inventing a more useful version of Christianity, run by Rome, to advance, with a unifying momentum, Emperor Constantine's agenda.

Empires fused politics with religion, to go after the faithful. Big religion was at war with God... Organized religion was run by Satan, not God. Watch out for state named religions.

In starkest contrast, is the evolution of the soul. Our soul lineage is mother-father-Maker. We move closer to our Maker as we move closer to ourselves.

We are born into the first breath of life. In communion with the root of our souls, we awaken into the higher breath of life. We are the sacrament of the three that are one. In alignment, we evolve into the fourth level of the soul. Living in confluence with the flow of the Sacred Wind, we awaken in ourselves, the higher breath of life.

Chapter Five
The Cleansing

W hen you go to church, synagogue or mosque, and God is not there, the derisive howl of demons, promise great destruction upon the land. The twin pillars, of freedom, are democracy and just law." Naomi was still transmitting.

"These pillars cannot hold and carry the dead weight of corruption. Those doors of freedom that slam, throughout history, are the most awful, and only the counterweight of faithfulness can open them again. The cure for tyranny is the Divine Presence.

"How can a structure last without its foundation? How can God Given freedom last, without God? Return to God, cleanse the Church and freedom will remain. Do it not, and darkness reigns. Until cleansed, the tree will bare false fruit. Until cleansed, how does freedom survive? Blinded by self-induced delusion, how does the vision of freedom remain?

"Living in confluence with the flow of the Sacred Wind bares wonderful fruit. Although this connection is below that of prophesy, it travels on the same wavelength. But first we need to cleanse from within, to make a difference. To bring back the power that the Church once had. To then go to the false church and drive a stake through the heart of a monster that derives its sustenance from iniquity. Sustaining the lust for wealth and power.

"To actually restore the public trust in our religious institutions. 'I would go to a church if I could find one.' How lonely, so many have been, wishing to establish a fellowship somewhere, where God still is. Some techniques can help draw you together. Reach up into the expansion, you will discover flying while standing in place. Be open and join in the opening. Stand in a circle with others and leap into standing flight, while holding hands to let the energy flow between you. The Sacred Wind will pulse with warm lifting energy, reaching in and through the focused clarity. We can become conductors of spiritual energy. Then sing together your songs of creation, holding hands still, and then see what happens. After, share with each other, what was experienced."

Looking back in American history, circa 2020, at the evil triumvirate of Vatican satellites, Italian and Swiss cloaking operations and Chinese puppet-master manipulations. Money bought the 2020 elections in America. This direct act of war was covered up by the political beneficiaries, who took office and continued selling out to the Chinese. Under this false rule trembled, those addicted to fear, with a need to rage, over nothing. There were two acts of war by China. The genetically engineered, bioweapon, released into the world as Covid19, and the computer engineered, cyber-hack-weapon used to steal elections.

The seeds of disunity were planted a long time before the seven-region brake-up occurred. Before the first civil war and so including, the red storm rising, of the Communist Revolution of 1917, in Russia, and 1927, in China. Core Church values stood there to oppose the storm. But then inexorably, the quest for wealth and power, began bleeding away, all the sacred virtue from within.

The churches couldn't get over themselves enough to trace the footsteps of the Messiah. They became the country clubs, of the self-righteous. The battle for evil stood, gradually unopposed. Exalting themselves rather than God, life and freedom, as they once had.

The Constitution, and the Bill of Rights, was by design, reflective of these core values. As these invaluable documents of freedom, lost their purpose, for the rising multitude of the godless, both in the Church and outside of it, our nation began blinding itself, by throwing out any such illumination.

Evil catastrophically unopposed. The Church no longer took responsibility. Our American Eagle began to fly away into the mountains, to the places where the faithful could be sustained. Judgement was at the door. It had not been a problem until the whole house of evil made it one. In tyranny lies only failure. The energy of truth is life giving energy. A humbling and cleansing tribulation came to rescue what was left, for those who remained true. Those battle worthy individuals, during the thousand-year conflict, found yet another chance to fly into battle and take the fight to Satan and win it!

During the Tribulation, protection was given to the sacred remnant, throughout the world. But when God's children became the whipping boy for evil, all hell broke loose. The Great Tribulation was man made. We chose to turn away. When we turned back, the tribulation ended, along with its childish tantrum against God. Another, Adam and Eve story, don't eat the apple, on a global scale. It had always been our responsibility. Whether we wind up in hell or heaven, is our choice. It is not God's plan, but ours! Bending down and lowering ourselves, to pick up off the ground, power, in its selfish form. Those who sought power, were infected with delusion, because ego morphs easily into infectious dead weight. The tribulation was Gods final battle on Earth, against evil, a global exorcism.

The Native American view is helpful to see all this clearly. The Great Awakening happens in the midst of total upheaval. It is the Great Blessing that is happening in the midst of the Great Tribulation. Bringing the return to connection with all that lives.

Whenever good people set out to defeat evil, it pleases Life

Giver, to get behind their resolute effort, letting them lead while flowing power to them, to seize their objective. Especially during The Great Tribulation, where partnership was most needed, to teach into the future, about the symbiotic relationship between God and man. Impeccable efforts moving in confluence, taking action together. History to this point, ran like a loop, in circles. Place-time repetitions on a regular basis. Einstein said doing the same thing, expecting different results was insanity and so, history was insane!

During the Great Tribulation, religious and spiritual organizations, were increasingly at war with their original belief charters. Any foundational keeping of their faith was under attack by these political-religious consortiums. They were out to destroy these sacred paths and ways of life, still practiced faithfully. Big religion was at war with God, sending their attack dogs to devour those of true heart. Organized religion was run by Satan, not God.

Empires fused politics with religion, to go after the faithful. Accordingly, Emperor Constantine circa 325AD, as the human architect of diabolical planning. To go after the faithful and seize power from God. Inventing a more useful version of Christianity, run by Rome, to advance, with a unifying momentum, Emperor Constantine's agenda. Then, eight hundred years later, Saint Augustine sealed the deal, betraying God. Teaching that evil issues from God, rather than Satan. In order to perform His hidden and greater plan. To cause the hapless victims of evil, to blame God. Satan had his disinformation campaign to ruin any form of honesty. But to make God, a capricious, creator of evil, was the greatest of all lies.

History books were almost devoid of reality, smothered by the black ether, that puts the soul to sleep with lies and distortions. "Whom the gods, actually demons, seek to destroy, they first make blind."

Math is a universal language, but so is music and art and spirit. They could be added to the four elements. Feeling, music, art, spirit, light spectra, color, sound, smell, are these not elements as well? Life is a fundamental element and force.

Life and spirit, should, at the least, be added to earth, wind, fire and water.

Chapter Six
Into The Future

I t was now possible to go to any era and test the truth of the history books, ever more deeply, to see the distortions made by Satan, who was dead now, never to return. It was astonishing to see how little written history had to do with what actually happened. To rewrite, in truth, had a most instructive value. Too bad that actual history, was unavailable, to those who were about to make it. Reality had been the original shape shifter.

Telepathy had ended the practice of telling lies. Reality, elucidated through the elasticity of spacetime, set all the bullshit aflame. The ones called tellers, were the historians of the telling...like it is! Past, present and future were unencumbered of all falsehood. Historical falsehoods were the last vestige of Satan...except for all those who had been slaves on all those home worlds, where they had been twisted by torture, in some instances, for hundreds of thousands of years.

After "The Thousand" two bitter pills remained. That of the depopulated planets and stars. Worst still, on those planets and stars, were populations of those that survived, the slaves left behind! They had been given no choice, being kept under most severe confinement. Most had no idea of what was going on. Many had prayed for freedom. They also had need of freedom from all the psychological damage. These captives were told of the stakes of the final battles in the final conflict. For them, these were all hopeful stories. They had been totally broken.

The enormous job of helping to restore and revive these tortured souls was absolutely necessary and fast! A slave is a prisoner of grave evil. First, after clothing them and feeding them, was to teach them of all that happened. The truth began to set them free. Teachers and healers would be left behind, to hold the line against what had been done to them. After feeding, clothing and healing came the process of soul repair. For multiple trillions of ex slaves!

Life Giver left all that hard work to be done by the grateful survivors of The Thousand. Their luminous souls would reach into their torn souls, and eventually, everywhere. Although the slavers had been driven by hate, the singers were driven by love. The defiant slave master's rage came from their guilt, which they turned into hatred toward their victims.

Vast Armadas, with ships of enormous size, set forth to the rescue. They brought medicine, livestock and tools, to work side by side with these unfortunate neighbors of theirs. They had synthesizers and simulators on board to create food or whatever physical items they might need. Translators were given to every living soul encountered. The microwave simulators could produce energy of any kind needed. But it was the joyously loving energy, that the rescued, needed most of all. Most of them were experiencing love for the first time in their shattered lives. Millions of ships would serve trillions of slaves. Their nightmares were slowly subsiding, in the midst of the fun, in being free.

Unraveling eternal mysteries, to share with them, on their journey to spiritual adulthood. On their quest to discover the expansion of their vision, their own evolving lens. They also had their own planets and stars, left to them, to replenish their lands and evolving souls. Build a future inhabited by real justice. After the unspeakable injustice they had emerged from.

From their holocaust, from their concentration camps. They had many blessings over them. They were the surviving casualties of Life Givers war with evil. Those that once were ruled by evil, were preserved as surviving remnants. The shifting into the selfless service, enjoyed by all.

On another light, entirely new light spectra, from other dimensions, were seeping into the web of non-verbal, communications. New sound spectra, and dreams, built on the totality of web consciousness. Spectacular multidimensional symphonies, cascading the new colors, new sounds, and the combined confluence, of all the creative genius, among all species. Yes, every living soul, danced in the ever-deepening connection. Math is a universal language, but so is music and art and spirit. They could be added to the four elements. Feeling, music, art, spirit, light spectra, color, sound, smell, are these not elements as well? Life is a fundamental element and force. Life and spirit, should, at the least, be added to earth, wind, fire and water.

Some would insist that sex was also one of the elements. Certainly, they could all be called languages. Space craft built for war, were used for peaceful service. The last contention was righting the wrongs of slavery, but history cannot be made into something that it was not. Yet the newly brightening ex slaves were hearing these new "dream symphonies" and so tears of joy were cleansing their tragic past, with hope for a new dawning day. Their dreams magnified, in these euphoric symphonies. Inter and trans-dimensional, influence, also had their voices or languages.

The Sacred Wind moves from within us. To touch the mysteries that cannot be expressed in words, that so easily, are experienced. All living beings have been designed to be capable vessels of the innermost, by choice. To open takes only the longing to do so. To come closer, to connect in experience. Things we can touch have no permanence. The Eternal Sacred Wind speaks forever from within us.

Abraham was the first Jew. Over time, practices would be established, called Halacha: the way. Messiah would be a man like King David, who would rescue the people from tyrants, as their General and King. Jesus was a different kind of Messiah. His lighted path: Haderech. He would rescue the people from evil, surpassing any King. He would open the path directly to God. His followers were a sect of Judaism. Emperor Constantin invented Christianity.

Christ was a Greek word for Messiah. Romes' new world order and religion, was meant to sever the Jewish roots of their path. By including all religions, a vast Empire, could replace Jerusalem with Rome.

Chapter Seven
Ever Beyond

Sex can be like music. Sometimes referred to as making music together, and yet another form of communicating or language. Telepathic non-verbal, communication, has an endless quality. Space was expanding at an ever-increasing velocity. Exploring all the new, habitable places, was an exhilarating fascination. And this became yet another vital new purpose for all those beings in spacecraft. They began settling new colonies with various species.

Adando and Mercuria were in fact having sex aboard one of those vessels. Their blue bodies undulating in euphoria. Their energies merging into a most beautiful symphony. Yes, sex can be experienced on multiple levels at once.

They had been ex slaves, now they were space explorers, with a real sense of the importance, in their mission. They entered into the places of the free, joining with all creation, in the joy of living.

When the present, overtakes a bitter past. Where love and life, fill in with sweet new memories. To let go of the bitterness of it. Transcending darkness by moving into the light.

Certain planets and stars were under a greater influence, by all the new, dimensional light, color, sound and somehow other, spectra. They were tracing them to see which planets and stars seemed to be influenced by location and dimension. Learning exponentially and constantly, whether asleep or awake. To be able to communicate with all living beings.

Oh, also, all the newly created sentient beings in constantly new, habitable places. No living, physical being could possibly keep track of it all. Where the soul leads, Divine pathways may be found. Adando and Mercuria were studying Earths history. Their conversation was currently about slavery in its many forms.

Mercuria, "Communism is slavery. Its victims were forced to work for the whims of the super state. Its mandate was to make war against any country that wished to live free. Freedom is the ultimate enemy of communism, which forces bondage to a will other than their own."

Adando, "We have fresh memory of this. Any government that denies the right to personal liberty, to make choices of their own, was parasitic slavery. Socialism was the path to fascism and communism, which made great bedfellows for each other, like Russia and China. Their common goal was coercion and force."

Mercuria, "War was their primary product, but controlling others is always to plant the seeds of war! Because our natural condition is liberty. Normal beings just want to be free. To create and keep what is their own. Giving voluntary generosity to whom they choose. Their religions were a representation of their souls."

Adando, "With cultures based on generosity, not licentiousness. But those entrapped by socialism fall down the slippery slope of ever greater force. Their religion was communism and fascism. Toward systematic, total control, by clever megalomaniacs. Seducing their already panic stricken populous. To jump into a technocracy, of total global micro-management. Rewarding or punishing behavior, of their human-robotic victims, where cash is no more!"

Mercuria, "Now our culture is based on the joy of providing for others, as all living beings have become neighbors and family members. So that no, is rarely spoken, in our tribal connectedness."

Adando, "Unity at the core of all life."

"The total unity of all that lives, receives sustenance from the Absolute Unity of Life Giver." Flux, the great Nomiruan Prophet, was captain of all the ships exploring the endless expansion. Yael and Ruarie lived on Nomiru and were married to

Nomiruans. They and Adando and Mercuria, were also in the lead ship with Flux, an amazing treat.

Some of the slave owning planets and stars had fought Alliance troops, who were there to clean out this profound evil. Therefore, many ex slaves were searching for new home worlds to get away from the enormous devastation that they had been left behind with. Much of it emotional. Justice for them was every one's problem until justice was delivered. Belief systems based in freedom, demanded this.

She would elucidate simply and patiently, sometimes playfully. Yael had an ancient Torah scroll. Jewish services were held on many ships in the year 48 BT, beyond time. The Jewish people would live forever, millions like Yael would see to it. To fully understand the Second and Third Testament, it was necessary to have the grounding of the First Testament. The foundation stone of the beginning, to walk the sacred path.

"To touch the mysteries that cannot be expressed in words, that so easily, are experienced. The Sacred Wind moves from within us. All living beings have been designed to be capable vessels of the innermost, by choice. To open takes only the longing to do so. To come closer, to connect in experience. Things we can touch have no permanence. The Eternal Sacred Wind speaks forever from within us." Yael was always inspiring, as a woman of valor.

The history of Israel and their walk with God, was revelation to the more evolved species. To them, past-present-future, were stacked and seen through as one, by the elasticity of time. Easily understood for them, was the concept that a relatively recent, pivotal time, like the birth of Messiah, was in fact at the beginning, of God's purpose. Life Giver chose to focus on them, so that the least would be first, by the Hand and Name of the Creator. All living beings could see how the point of origin, for all existence, came from one single source: that of Life Giver,

Messiah and Sacred Wind. With Messiah as the Imminent Hand of The Absolute. His Hand in creation, from a God's eye view.

Yael, "Jesus was not a Christian, He was a Jewish man, like Moses or Elijah, only more. We can only see as much of this as we are able, as we continue on this path. That Jesus was God's Hand in creation. Many of the more evolved species came to witness, invisibly, along with the three wise men from the east, the birth of Messiah. Our vessel grows in dimensionality, walking this path. The euphoric light of life keeps expanding from within us. Messiah, made in God's image and likeness, from the beginning.

"My ancestor Jake once said," "If you are afraid, then you are already dead. In the center of the canvas of history, are the Jewish people. The Jews knew tribulation many times. To be killed, enslaved and driven from their home. Whenever world powers arise, they always arise in the force of fascistic empire. Whenever empires have Jews, dictators attack them. Those who by their connection with God, challenge their power.

"Just in recent history, modern day powers resembling ancient Egypt or ancient Rome, have made great tribulations, for the Jewish people. Paradigm for the renewed Roman Empire. Like that of the Third Reich in the time of Hitler, or that of the next empire, of the next and final Antichrist, and his next occupation of Israel and slaughter of the Jews, in the Great Tribulation.

"Satan requires the world powers to kill his enemy, the Jews and Christians. All those of Sacral Covenant, are in the way, of his quest for power over all the Earth. America rose to power, by God's Blessings and while America was refuge for Jews and Christians, they prospered. The Great Tribulation left no such refuge. The last shoe to drop." Yael spoke through her tears, "That pretty much says it all. Am Yisrael Chai." The people Israel live.

To live and grow and reproduce and love, were of primary natural law. Ever since the beginning of life, this was to see God, and live. To look around the natural world and literally see God. That God had myriad elements, manifestations, levels and dimensions. As Life Giver inhabits all existence. Growing the lens to see, that life is the primary element, of the so called four. That were actually six: Life, Spirit, Earth, Wind, Fire and Water.

Flux had a night vision. Of a people, in a distant time, called Brahim. Of one called Amaliah. His fierce love for a woman called Eliah. From a people called Divine Reckoning. Both descended from ancient Jewish roots.

Both wildly handsome and tall. He, raven haired with dark green eyes. An incredible beauty, she had stunning bright copper eyes. Fiery red hair. Lovely, soft skin, in a light golden-yellow hue.

She felt his gaze upon her from across the room. Not only a libidinous attraction, he felt love deeply for her. She could feel this vividly! His telepathic voice began whispering to her, "You are life to me." Elegantly simple, she answered, "I feel you. I see you."

Chapter Eight
Surprise!

The perfect jewel was before them. Ships began landing, on the fascinatingly beautiful paradise. While other ships continued making their studies from within the atmosphere while still airborne. This huge star seemed perfect. There was a population of sentient beings, gentle, shy and quiet. Seemingly early in their evolution and no threat to the settlement of new colonies. Mercuria sang out joyously, "Feels like home to me." Physically, we see to believe, spiritually, we believe to see. For everyone at once, believing was seeing.

This star was definitely influenced by other dimensions. Light, color, sound, smell, taste and the way of seeing. Something like the Gods Touch places were within sight for those airborne, but they were a symphony of blazing and brilliant pastels. There were base colors other than just red, yellow and blue but names for these new colors had not yet been given. Delightful to behold, a natural sense of well being permeated. They were yet to meet the other sentient beings. Their intelligence was phenomenal. Newly created, but capable of learning on every level, at a velocity to rival or exceed any other known being. Gentle and kind and most eager to come close and touch their fellow beings, with an innocence and openness that brought tears of joy to the explorers, who then began to return their touching embrace.

A star of momentous significance to all. To become a learning place for all.

They walked upright with three fingers and a thumb. Their heads were large in the back of their cranium and high in their forward cranium. Two huge eyes of grey with pupil and iris, that had many colors swirling and sparkling in a black background.

They had no hair on their athletic bodies, which were partly covered by a kind of cloth made from woven fiber, making generous robes.

Their skin was multi-translucent, with brilliant rainbows of constantly shifting colors, which seemed to express some kinds of emotion, but their minds were so powerful.

They had the appearance of a profoundly inquisitive, deeply sensitive nature. They had no wings but that did not stop them from showing up anywhere. The depth of their intelligence seemed unfathomable. They would have appeared to be as gods to those who did not know there was only One. Their eyes were full of kindness. In their language, they were called Lysandrum.

Flux, "A newly created being, starting out at this level of evolution, has never been heard of, so far as I know. Let's see if they can be on the web, by simply telling of it, in our wordless speaking. We'll have to because they seem to be beyond our translator devices. Wow, now I see! They are already on the web, their telepathic ability is amazing, they can hold multiple conversations at once. By the velocity of their thought. They are past us all, yet they are newborn children."

Back inside the ship, Ruarie was holding forth to a bunch of little children, on the histories of the worlds. Earth was a good starting point, as good and evil seemed, so totally out of their human control. Evil was hard to understand, why would anyone want yucky stuff?

These children, of many species, had hugely voracious curiosity and their nonverbal transmissions could be overwhelming.

"Kids, please, let's go vocal, without any other transmissions. So, our focus, can be less overwhelming to me. Some of your brains are too powerful for me." Certain species, even when tiny children, were gifted in the extreme. Their telepathy could drown out any and everyone else. Their mental energies could humble others.

"Evil, the Adversary, Satan and his hordes of hell, would never be over until completely eradicated. A harmful enemy, that must be entirely killed to stop it. Because it is the most infectious disease of all. One that feeds on fear and torment, while tearing and feeding on the soul, our interior light source. Advanced disease was called possession. Its breeding ground is ego, the first one infected was Lucifer, the so called, Angel of Light."

"An exorcism is a battle to remove one demon or more, from the soul that has been infected. A battle between God and Satan, that is initiated by an exorcist, the person who takes action, to deliver justice, on behalf of the living being, whose own will, has been taken over.

"The tormented being, who wants to be free, welcomes the battle, not unlike surgery only scarier. The incense, Holy Water and powerfully fervent prayers, give severe torment to the demon. Enough so, that the parasitic demon is split between his duty to Satan and his desire to escape.

"But it is not the exorcist who drives out the demon. The tug of war is between the will of God and the will of Satan. By the exorcist taking action, to deliver a being from torment, God is called to inspiration, empowering the exorcism. It gets ugly because Satan is thwarted, and demons are called to the battle. But it is the covenant of heavenly empowerment, that calls the Angels to the conflict, and looses the demon from the soul he has been feeding on. The demon must then go hunting for his next meal. Demons are soul eaters."

"Wouldn't it be simpler to ask for Life Givers light to surround a living being with the light of creation?" A tiny kid with big know how. "Absolutely, darling child!" She was crying, as this simplicity and clarity was a most dazzlingly, wondrous, sight to behold. Her tears were most instructive to her students.

Now, back outside of the ship, a festival was taking place, to give thanks for all the visitors. Similar festivities celebrating the arrival of the explorers, were happening all over the huge star. The Lysandrum were very grateful and inviting. They were loving beings!

On multiple levels, breaking the "rules of reality" to set things right, came the flood of understanding to the previously unheard of. The Lysandrum would at times, in the embraces of several together, bring on a quicksilver light show, that would break out passionately. From their own essential attributes. The brightness thrilled all to see. They had no appetite to be intoxicated. Their natural state could easily build euphoria both stronger and deeper.

Their music was based on sounds unusual to the ear of a visitor. Their skins undulating colors, as well as their eyes, would shift harmonically, to the sounds of their music. These skin and eye tones had colors no stranger had ever seen. Their very presence had a spectacular flavor, unlikely to be dreamed of, as they were truly unusual.

But Flux had seen them. "My dreams were emotional and always left my pillow wet with happy tears. Feeling that these new beings would have a strong influence in our tribal culture, far and wide, endlessly expanding. Our total tribal unity culture would be blessed by the special light of these wondrous newborn beings."

To name a new color, first we must see it. To write music with new sounds, we must hear them. All the many senses and feelings would need new language to describe them. It was clear that these newborn beings would change everything. They could teleport, so why fly, unless for fun. As the technologies from the outside worlds were absorbed, explosions of discovery would arrive in vast floods for them. Then to be shared on the Web.

Seeing a wonder for the first time brought inspiration in a feedback loop between all species, especially the newly created. Eyes would dance with light at first encounter with the Lysandrum. All living beings were set to accelerate their development ever faster. This was just another example, that the primary element, is life and its light. To live and grow and reproduce and love, were of primary natural law. Ever since the beginning of life, this was to see God, and live. To look around the natural world and literally see God. That God had myriad elements, manifestations, levels and dimensions. As Life Giver inhabits all existence. Growing the lens to see, that life is the primary element, of the so called four. That were actually six: Life, Spirit, Earth, Wind, Fire and Water.

When they teleported, all their swirling colors began shifting about, and just before takeoff, a bright, mercurial, sheen, would suddenly begin to disappear them. Now one more startling difference was apparent. They would go from the dark gemstone colors of intention, to ever lightening pastel colors of opening, to brightly lighter silver colors of expansion, to a take off of shining brightness of no color, to a sudden disappearance. The last thing that could be seen of them, before they left, were their dreaming body ghosts, and eyes that could see to any distance. They were to revolutionize the way we could experience.

Life Giver's presence, we feel. We return His love with all we have within us. He is within us and inhabits every living thing. The Habitation of Existence is His name. As inside all that is, His heart is our heart, in union.

As it is that our song, He sings, with love. In all His loving creation, new worlds are being made, in His image, to the reaches of eternity. New worlds, that increasingly reflect, His Sword of Truth. Having sung His song of creation. In His own language, tenderly, but with all His might. Taking us into the thrall of perfect unity. To stand in the midst of eternity, joyously.

God sings to us, His songs of creation. Our interior is infinite and constantly expanding like the exterior endless expanse.

Chapter Nine
Cloud Spectra

Several thousand settlers chose to stay. So many that a few ships would be left behind with them. All who stayed were explorers of the unseen newness. No different than those who traveled on. Nearly a thousand Lysandrum took the leap, inside the exploring ships. They were sure to revolutionize the experiential way of all the crew members. What a blast for all, those staying and those leaving.

The Eritraian and Lysandrum on board, upgraded the translators to include the very musical, rhythmic language of the Lysandrum, who gave quite a light show while speaking. Their name translates in English, as Alive Ones. They were teleporting busily, learning, teaching and visiting. In short order, they had learned a majority of languages and taught theirs to millions. The Alive Ones were now in deep communion, on telepathic web. Sometimes, they would get excited and teleport, so they could be physically in touch with whomever had inspired them.

Soon they were living on a whole lot of home worlds. They were invited and welcomed with fervor. Their communications inundated web consciousness dramatically. They would get together with Howan Beings and Nomiruans, to sing and dance. The experience of these celebrations reverberated to the far reaches, with a dynamic, joyful, resonance.

All this made one thing clear as could be. Spiritual Inner-Tech could surpass any other means, by a long shot. The vast innermost, was the place, where thought could become reality. To speak it into being, as a lesser mirror, of how the Creator speaks into existence, what He desires to create. Our interior is infinite and constantly expanding like the exterior endless expanse.

This was the spot where the Alive Ones truly shined! They, in their primal, newborn state, found abilities potentiate to them. By teaching and training themselves, from scratch! They were alive from deep within. Their name for Life Giver was Father Life. The intersection where all the living meet.

As Magdalyn Lightkeeper led the service, being held for all living beings at once, Ordaryn began to sing, from the depths of his soul. "Life Giver's presence, we feel. We return His love with all we have within us. He is within us and inhabits every living thing. The Habitation of Existence is His name. As inside all that is, His heart is our heart, in union.

"As it is that our song, He sings, with love. In all His loving creation, new worlds are being made, in His image, to the reaches of eternity. New worlds, that increasingly reflect, His Sword of Truth. Having sung His song of creation. In His own language, tenderly, but with all His might. Taking us into the thrall of perfect unity. To stand in the midst of eternity, joyously.

"Our love songs, to Father Life. Touching creations power of life. Hearing God's love song to us. Creating in constancy, with His Voice, we all can hear." In the language of the Lysandrum, it sounded more wonderful than the English translations.

The Alive Ones led some of these connection services, telepathically throughout the web expanse, to all living beings. They brought a current of ecstatic splendor, wherever they were, to touch the flow of life that reached everywhere.

Constant change is an element, of the essence of life. The Ultimate Reality is Life Giver. His essence is spiritually expressed and genetically encoded, in all evolving creation. All creation reflects His Attributes: "His Face." We are not just "meat popsicles," we are also Divine conduits, flowing Divine Energies.

Few recognized, something readily apparent, to the student of Jewish Kabbalah. How, in a way, we might see Creator, by assembling created. That taken together, all of us, like pieces in a jigsaw puzzle, could picture a reflection of our Creator. Or the image of God, like a mirror, when broken and the shards of broken mirror are brought together, that of all living souls, could finally provide reflection, of the Ultimate Soul: the true image of God's "Face."

Chapter Ten
Begin Again Forever

Alyra, of the Photochai, the Living Picture beings, were of an emerald green, with loud neon black stripes. "From infinite possibilities, we decide who we are, in the ease and simplicity of our inner multiverse. Concepts like future and past, melt into present reality, as we go both ways at will. As we merge into our present-future-past, our pathways to the living light open to reality as it is, in the completed present. Beyond place-time outward-inward, to begin again, once more."

Their jungle planet, of medium size, was rich in wildlife. Jaguar like, were these Living Picture Ones. Rich, black soil, heavy rainfall, and a constant celebration of being alive. Thousands of explorers leaped for the chance of knowing them. It was always this way. They had three Suns, five Moons and many other sundrenched planets nearby. They were born with the ability of spacetime travel as well as dimensional travel. Born this way, like the Lysandrum!

In the "year" of 371 BT, all large scale, resettlement of the once enslaved, always free, had been accomplished, leaving behind a bitter vacuum. The number of new home worlds had expanded so quickly that nearly all onetime Alliance craft were fully deployed to gain, in the new and timeless alliance unfolding at phenomenal velocity. Humongous new craft were out there exploring all the new and exciting treasures of creation, like seeing a new part of God all the "time."

New populations were greater than "old" ones. The phantasmagoria of enlightening, inspiring, new contact, kept an open embrace filled to overflowing. The experience, of infinity, gave deep meaning to the word, that was Life Giver. With the endless wonder of touching so many new examples of Apex, newly born, species. Amid the always enveloping from within, of total unity. The organizing faculty of unity without end, by the loving Hand of Creator. As the unaccepted, Apostle, Thomas said, "The Kingdom of God is within you." This flew in the face of total church control by suggesting we take responsibility ourselves.

With so much freedom from the pressure of eking out a "living," "time," was available to explore. All living souls were avid explorers, because each new species was another facet of God's "face." Another picture of how Life Giver feels, from the passion of His creation.

These newly created species had, woven into them, profound gifting. By their very nature, they had been created, to open endless doors, of both perception and capability. To inform the greater picture of how it is! Their gifts could not be mimicked, because they were structural and native to the totality of inherited qualities, that were given them by design. Genetic qualities, like the Alive Ones and the Living Picture Ones had, could not be cloned or reproduced, because their total architecture could only be known by their Creator, who wanted all beings to find their own unique way, because the effort for their discoveries, were healthy for them. By their own virtue, do they find, and their virtue, is what they find.

Ever shifting, the elasticity of time, illustrated fluidity in timelessness. After the Thousand, it became clearer by the day, that home world advancements, through the prism of web consciousness everywhere, were soon up to speed, "in no time." In endless space, the only limit, was in how fast explorers could arrive, in the explosion of discovery. Many of these unknown species were giving and receiving web transmissions long before physical visits occurred.

Differences in abilities were the only differential. Howan Beings, Human Beings, the Nomiruan, Eritraian, Lysandrum,

Photochai and innumerable others, had within them, gifting that reached toward some ultimate quality.

Few recognized, something readily apparent, to the student of Jewish Kabbalah. How, in a way, we might see Creator, by assembling created. That taken together, all of us, like pieces in a jigsaw puzzle, could picture a reflection of our Creator. Or the image of God, like a mirror, when broken and the shards of broken mirror are brought together, that of all living souls, could finally provide reflection, of the Ultimate Soul: the true image of God's "face."

Life Giver did see it that way. A part of His soul's essence, in every created being. He was creating ever new species, that taken together, could possibly comprise, in some measure, an accurate picture, of the Architect, Himself. In some ultimate future, all living beings in their physical assemblage, would reflect the spiritual image of the One, who made them all. This had always been the way of it, but someday, much more.

But they would never merge to become one. Physical facsimiles were necessary to contain absolute unity. Though as one in a living dynamic unity, no merging to the relative erasure of the living physical could be done without destroying full dimensionality.

On another note, there was a Divine Exorcism, driving out the master demon Satan, from his parasitism of planet Earth. The Thousand was the next exorcism, of the endless expanse. Satan feared we might someday take responsibility for our relationship with Life Giver, see through his divisive artifice, and give him the boot!

Because Messiah is the Living Hand of Creation, He is the beginning. Life Giver chose a primal people, taken directly from Him, for the location of His physical birth in Israel. The Mystery of Creation begins here, in God's Eternal plan. With Father creating through Son, at the absolute beginning, eons before. God moves beyond the timelines of His creation. With His Spiritual Son, at creations beginning, and then much later, the fused-material-spiritual-Messiah, born in Israel, with a physical body like ours.

Constant change is an element, of the essence of life. The Ultimate Reality is Life Giver. His essence is spiritually expressed and genetically encoded, in all evolving creation. All creation reflects His Attributes: "His Face." We are not just "meat popsicles," we are also Divine conduits, flowing Divine Energies.

After Satan, an entirely new limitless reality replaced the one limited by Satanic intrusion. This reality made possible by the removal of evil. With evil gone it was still necessary, for all of us, as students of history, to see the full demonic possession that all existence had been subjected to. The contrasting shift from that to complete liberation was, in the wink of an eye, a wonder to behold. Freedom makes it possible for the lion to lay down with the lamb, if not physically, at least metaphorically, as meat was still food to many living creatures. However, war was no more.

To another subject, there were never enough Spanish Kiger Horses. They now had longer legs and were more uphill in conformation, making them smoother than ever. Their unique markings, zebra like, were now more pronounced than ever, neon black leaping to meet the eye, against a mouse colored background. Hotblooded wonders of intelligence and most willing to bond with their rider. Companionship and affection easily gifted in a feedback loop of mutual love and respect. There will always be horsemen! There will always be fine Spanish horses.

Favored critters from various home worlds were shared universally. Why teleport when you can ride a horse to go fishing? Disease, politics, religion, war, subjugation and bondage were gone forever, along with hunger, fear, jealousy and hate. If anything, reproductive impulses had risen enormously. Along with emotion, art in every form and music in particular. New sounds, colors, and light spectra, all aided the greater exuberance. To play was considered a most valuable enterprise.

Dreamers were encouraged. Sharing between cultures and travel everywhere, both newly discovered and already beloved. Living in celebration of the vast riches everywhere, to behold in the experience of them.

Freedom was deeply revered by all, as the greatest gift ever given, for in it was life itself. Its central value to God was the result of its necessity for life. The elemental power of life. But to explore, including history, was now, like a prayer, the greatest task of any living being. Gone forever, scarcity, replaced by abundance. God loves to give as we do. A celebration of giving was now constant. Facing up to the past, however, was still necessary. Some of it, so bleak and grim.

Shifting now toward a dark vacuum of the ancient past. The children were studying primitive cultures. They zoomed in by remote viewing, to see and hear the beastly chatter, of disrespect and vicious disunity. The children were appalled. 2020 AD, America, was a study in evil, comprised of an orgy, in trying to steal power and control from each other. As ugly as any time in Earth's history. A precious few, a remnant, still found courage in their faith. They understood that a planet-killer-war, was beginning.

For the rest, it was always about who gets more and having the power to subjugate others. These malignant distortions led to war, always, throughout Human history. Their hatred and indifference to all but their coconspirators, trying to steal power and control, by whatever hellish means required.

Their hatred key, in the battle for political power over each other, was destroying any hope for democracy. That which both sides claimed to hold as paramount. But they were utterly false.

God, life and freedom meant nothing to most of them. Stealing elections was proof positive, of that!

Their divisions drove them, into political and economic collapse. Their ethics were lost completely. The vacuum of leadership, fed global power struggles, triggering the Great Tribulation. In blindness, they could not picture the unity of all that lives, with mutual love and respect.

An angry man shouted, "The ones who wash black with blood red, and call it grey, are thieves of freedom. They were always meant to be dead. In the Art of War, Sun Tzu wrote, 'Fight the enemy where they are not.' Insert confusion and moral unclarity and watch the dummies gobble up the lies. Entertain the masses, while brainwashing them."

An angry woman agreed, "Such bitter irony, with the pots of chaos boiling over. Any violence coming out of election disputes, will only fuel the furnace of Fascism. Because violent upheaval is always met with crushing government control. Shots fired will sound the death knell of our fragile democracy, no matter which side wins."

One of the children in history class, spoke with tears in her eyes, "Those Earthers seemed a lot dumber than the ones we have now." Another child, "It is because the survivors, that saw their way through the darkness, lived on, evolved, and passed their virtue, on to their progeny."

Back in 2024, a man said, "You only win if you survive. Not every battle, but the war." Behind every lie, is demonic influence. History was a minefield, of lies.

All the new history books included the endless number of exclusions, by those in power. For example, in the Rocky Mountains of America, early in the year 2024, a major battle, leaving astonishing results, was prosecuted by government forces. The uneven casualties were seemingly impossible.

A huge bivouac, of standing forces, had gathered on a day, in a large mountain valley, to eradicate the freedom fighters. They were townsfolk, loggers, miners, farmers and ranchers. They knew these mountains. Fireteams began to harry, by sniper fire, the huge army gathered against them.

Their targets were drones, officers, squad gunners, radio operators and artillery crew. As they were closed against by massive waves of government forces using suppression fire, the partisans continued to move back into the remote hiddenness, while engaging each new wave with accurate precision fire. A fine battle plan, made by a fine soldier, who had served in Detachment One, an outfit like Delta, from which they had drawn their best. He was one of the architects, tactically, who designed victory. Many great soldiers were with the partisans.

Soon most of the occupying forces were fighting under the canopy of dense forest. The partisans had set thousands of ambushes that the government forces were falling into. Fierce levels of bombardment from the air and stand off artillery, continued to fall on partisans and occupiers alike. The forest fires were then started way back where the fighting had begun. Mountain sheer winds blew uphill, giving powerful momentum to the firestorm. Then the fires were making their own weather and raging up toward the incline where the fighting also raged. Deer rifles against a modern army. They had underestimated the spirit of the resolute citizenry.

Wave after wave of government forces advanced up the higher elevations. They were killed by the thousands while thousands of partisans let them chase them, until they caught them. Finally, the partisans dispersed in retreat, throughout vast areas of remote mountains. The fires continued to chase hundreds of thousands of weary government forces. The fires killed more of them, than the riflemen had.

The freedom fighters lost over seventeen thousand killed.

Army losses of two hundred and thirty-two thousand, killed by combat and the firestorm, set by determined beginners. Nothing was reported. None of it was known, in the news or the history books. But these deliberate, resolute, men, women and children prevailed, through the might of the spirit. Called the lollapalooza, by the free people. Word of mouth sent thrills of encouragement to the resistance. Historians, of that time, would not touch it, with a ten-foot pole. The children that saw this in their history class were deeply saddened. Actual history was very sad.

Trust is the most valuable, Human commodity. Trust of Life Giver and trust of each other. With that trust comes love. From that love comes life. Within that life is the light of creation. To elevate oneself, is to fall from being the vessel, that relies on walking along the Lords' path. To wait upon His guidance and see their purpose. This is what basic spiritual physics looks like.

As your day goes by, turn to Him, who has sought you. In your time passing, reach out to Him, Who, gives life. In His pursuit of You, receive Him. While you walk, turn back to Him, He will surely turn back to you. For your thirst, His living waters. Drink from His well and He will accompany you, throughout your life.

God is, life and freedom. Our souls are the focus, of the interior light of creation.

Chapter Eleven
Celestial Rhythm

The souls embrace, reaching out to any soul, longing for greater communion, puts us all deeply in touch with each other. With remote viewing, physical contact was simulated, as a result of sharing all of the senses, between few or many, by choice. Intimacy was found by focusing these communications, solely between those desired. An absolute openness could be pictured, thus opening to every living soul. Our souls are the focus of the interior light of creation, so that inner technology had an endless lamp, to wish, see and then create, the vessel for making things happen.

A perfect Celestial Rhythm established, between trillions of trillions of souls. In a dynamic, harmonic, musical, rhythmic, resonance. A conversation of blessed exchange. Where every gift of loving contact, is given with the desire to return still greater generosity of the spirit. Of dwelling most high among those resolute to give. As a joy to do so. As a symptom of love, nearing the far reaches of the heart. More magnificent than the stars and planets abounding. Way beyond just a universe in its reach.

For a finite being version of perfection mirrored, from their picture of what the Infinite One's might be. Love is the ultimate, universal language. It is the language that Life Giver lives and creates by. One of the instruments playing, in His song of creation. Every living soul is drawn together by it. Drawn together in unity. Embraced by the Absolute Unity, that has created it. This conversation blessed by the One of All.

The next encounter took place when the Flux-led armada went searching quite a bit further than ever before, in relation to any other known population. This time, no one expected to be caught in the thrall of wonder like this. First, a Gods Touch area larger than ever before seen, seemed to herald, something entirely unusual. The arousal of Gods Touch energies left them openly enhanced and ready. The clouds were so thick, nothing could be seen.

Down to a thousand-foot elevation, they moved carefully, by instruments, until the light flashed in the clouds, with staggering levels of creamy luminescence. But still, at five-hundred feet, nothing. Then suddenly in the brilliance of colors in the vegetation, loomed flying creatures, with plumage almost too bright to see clearly. Colors so vivid as to amaze the eye.

Scientific and technological discoveries are easily eclipsed by native capabilities, when stretched toward their unknown limits. Beings in dynamic-creative-evolution, helped by their Maker, can do whatever they imagine, in the opening they make through connection. Still the opening they would witness, went past what they could imagine.

After the ships landed, the crews were stunned. Standing before them at every landing, were beings seemingly more Angelic than other species. Their bodies were corporeal while shifting to a somehow incorporeal version. Two or more in one. They were electric white, with light grey eyes. They appeared to be, incongruently, an intelligence deeper in inner brilliance than met before. Created quite recently, they were already the most advanced physical beings known. Advanced in ways not as yet, or maybe, never understood.

Their two forms oscillated constantly. With the more ghostly side flashing at perfect intervals, at velocities surpassing lightning. At these times, the ozone like that after a lightning strike, made the air more moist and delightful to breathe. Leaving, a health giving, balance, in the wake, and a dramatically heightened sense of wellbeing. They were more than friendly, tender, toward the many different species greeting them. Feeling joy often, looking up and out, with tears of gratitude in their large eyes.

64

Although partly physical, their insights and revelations were close to that of an Archangel. Their interior light, like that of the soul, filled their bodies. Flux emotionally spoke a truth none could argue.

"They, the whole of them, are a soul! Their inner light, that of the soul, is constantly expressed, throughout their totality. In their entirety, they are what we hold in our core essence, within us, our souls. The most luminous light of the soul. They are what we have within us. In their synaptic transfer, between their two states, oscillations move clockwise, in synch with the orbit of their planet, just like our souls, but their souls are big enough to fill their whole bodies. Their mercurial light, quietly explodes, from within them, in their serenity. Seemingly like some missing link between Creator and created.

"Their powers are beyond our understanding. Perhaps even beyond their own. Their presence is a rhapsody, in depth. Being both heavenly and earthly. Making weather they say let it rain, that's what those clouds were about, it made them laugh at how surprised their visitors would suddenly be. They were playing with us.

"They wanted us to understand that they can change most anything at will. Stop a forest fire, or turn it in the right direction, for the ideal benefit of the wildlife there. These powers were known by Earth's Adam and Eve, but are not conditioned on proper behavior, as they were. They have arrived at these powers from within their vary nature.

"The Scintillae hear all of us at once. They respond to all of us at once. We must leave many tens of thousands here, from among our known species. To commune with them and evolve with them."

Flux, crying with joy, began to dance, the Scintillae joined us, along with all the rest of the crews leaping in as well.

This "day" named the Day of Light, marked by the historians, of every living being. Multiple tens of thousands of the Scintillae would also settle off world. Wherever they traveled, a delight to meet them. On the roll call of expanding creation.

While they were dancing, by the sounds of their hauntingly evocative instruments, the Scintillae grew brighter and then came, a refinement of counter melodies harmonizing. These melodies came from them, like instruments inside them. They seemed to be more abreast of all knowledge, than other species. They showed their guests altogether breakthrough colors, sounds, light spectra and like the Howan, practice all forms of lovemaking in scintillating harmony.

Still, there was much about them, that could not be described in words, no matter what language. But they might have the words for some of it. Their planet was huge and rich in whatever any being might need. They had room to spare and millions would come to live with them. Room to spare on all planets and stars, which outnumbered all the sentient beings out there.

They had no buildings. Their control of the weather was complete, so that they had never wanted houses, that would inhibit their total experience with all that was out there. They wore minimal clothing for the same reason. Always festive and ready to celebrate.

A large bunch of little kids were speaking together, around the fire. "A couple thousand years ago, on Earth, discoveries were made, that enabled craft to avoid collision with all the barriers like asteroids, both huge and tiny."

"The shielding they developed, moved objects and particles, out of the way, as they sped through their vast beginning of exploration. Otherwise, we would have a tiny particle, hit by a ship moving more than fast enough to easily explode the ship."

"This, resistance displacement system, moved space from the front leading edge of the ship to its back, along with whatever else, and thus tremendous gains in velocity could be attained. It redirected potential impact situations nicely, while providing a slingshot effect with considerable gains in performance."

"Those primitive ships, piloted by primitive 'Singers,' could perform well enough, to win the war with evil. We must never forget what they have done for us. Fearless bravery, like a sacrament, to provide justice, wherever they were guided to go."

Little kids with big brains. Then those marvelous flying creatures swooped down to visit with the children. They were birdlike, and tremendously intelligent. Their colors were a dark neon, intensely bright, like gemstones. But they had big eyes and wanted to play with the children. And play they did.

The Scintillae, which translates as the 'In light Ones,' had no leaders. An old book about the Singers, was presented to their entire population, of nearly one billion. Once all who read it, returned it to Flux, he had a library built, for them to keep it. It would enshrine the courage of the many stouthearted ancients. Logs of the musings of so many great Singers, kept on their lifelong tours of duty. Many copies were made. For example, Benjamin. From his writings entitled, "The Good Ship Lollypop," some excerpts.

"As your day goes by, turn to Him, who has sought you. In your time passing, reach out to Him, Who, gives life. In His pursuit of You, receive Him. While you walk, turn back to Him, He will surely turn back to you. For your thirst, His living waters. Drink from His well and He will accompany you, throughout your life.

"No prison can withhold the uncontainable triumph. I, Benjamin, the aborted and then resurrected son of both man and woman yet of God alone in my rebirth, have found and been given, His Way, in the halls of eternity. For my life, seemingly finite, has always been eternal.

"He enters all creation as His garden. Our souls live in the juncture of God and man. Dwelling within us and all around."

Created from His essence, our souls are part of Him, as His soul is part of us.

That is why the miraculous inhabits all He touches. That is why miracles are normal.

With our trust and service, He lights our path to perfect freedom.

Chapter Twelve
Follow The Light

Those vast reaches of darkness, where the light of suns, are rarely found, somehow lost the blinding effect of pitch black. No, not through thermal, shipboard devices, like before. In the vast, cold, dark, thermals were useless anyway. Except in seeing dark planets, to avoid slow velocity collision. At higher velocities, collision avoidance was handled by folding space. The phenomena that sends space and obstacles around the speeding airfoil.

God's face, to light the way, increased exponentially, as He drew near, as He had always done for those that relied upon Him. For those with the vessel to receive, He drew water from His well. In short, space was getting brighter.

Solary of the Brahim, "Could the presence of Heaven be drawing closer to us all? It seems as though everywhere is returning back to Him." His wife retorted, "Gee, honey, do you think so?" Teasing was common as we merged with the great, unending, beyond. 'Passing the time,' was an inadequate phrase. Perhaps passing the timeless, is closer to it. Endless quiet, expanding outward, still held us somewhat in awe.

However, we were not following the light. It was everywhere. The humbling realization here, is that the light is really following us, and that, as the result of our seeking it! And that, as the result of Life Giver seeking us. For a merger, that while keeping all creation distinct, it would nevertheless, keep dynamic intimacy. That most ancient of phrases, 'There is nothing but God,' might be put, 'There is nothing without God.'

Then suddenly, gradually, it began getting so bright that we were almost blinded by it. Solary said meditatively yet urgently,

"All consciousness aboard ship, let go and move with this, or we may not make it through these shifting dimensionalities. The danger is being left behind, for those hanging on too tightly. Focus on Life Giver." He had not mentioned the scary part about being left behind. How you could cease to exist. Left behind in nothingness.

A soul departure to nowhere left only erasure! Where the evil all went to, long ago. Fortunately, no one, was left behind. But these were as yet unknown dimensionalities. Flying Wreath of Realms, these were still radically new places. Requiring absolute trust, in order to see them. The act of letting go, in trust, is the dynamism required to get the whole picture. Finding actual reality is the grandest prize!

Beings were coming into view, but they were made of light...pure light! What language do you use, to communicate with pure light? Turns out, no language. Pure light just is. The 'conversation' is to experience it and to be experienced by it. Photographic but not physical. A camera could make the picture of it. This experience charged our batteries, our energy envelopes, in ways we were yet to discover. But to speak about the wordless is nearly impossible.

The real message was just to stand with them, be, with them. As our eyes and souls began to adjust to them, we began to feel their affection for us. We had crossed another border together, on our evolutionary trail. As we waved good-bye, their love was sending us on our way. Could it be that the greatest distances of all, were internal?

We could not remember our ships landing anywhere. Our ships logs showed that we had not. We just showed up. Or they arranged for us to meet with them somewhere. But where in the heck? Had we become nonphysical, or partly so? Were they? Or did we go together to meet in our togetherness. We laughed because what ever it was, it was wondrously the best. We did not need to over think it. It just was, and we were glad for it. We laughed ever onward, on the odyssey, to everywhere.

We did crave to stand on the living, breathing ground again. Hyperspace on hyperdrive, returned us quickly. Like Vikings on magic boats, we returned laden with treasure. It was always so good to be home. Wanderlust, fortunately for us, was not constant. Our treasured adventures paled before the treasure of home.

Many of the married couples were with child and nesting was a priority. There is no place like home. We expand more at home and through our dreams, than we do by hauling ass into the even more unknown. The Brahim are a roving species, but we are also a coming home species. Warriors in love with peace.

Another form of travel was ancestral travel. These excursions bore sweetest fruit.   For in the halls of life beyond time, grow the trees of ancestry. Where our ancestors are alive as ever, with open arms. Aundeiri was over fourteen thousand years old, in the prime of his adulthood. Anciently, this time came at forty, the time to study the mysteries, Kabbalah. Some ancestors are reborn to the Heavens, while some are resurrected, to finish their work. But the ancestral living trees, are the when and where of what has been, what may be. To know them in their own beginnings, was the purpose of returning to them, in their ancestral tree. One can also visit their tree, of the knowledge of good and evil, for perspective. How they fulfilled their purpose, relative to that.

Aundeiri would make the journey to meet them all, to eat the purple flower. Dreaming across the waters of life. To join with them. To see and feel them on every branch of the ever- living tree of life, of his people.

He would also visit the tree of those to come, especially his wife and children, and their progeny. Without time suspension these journeys might last centuries. When he was done, it would feel to him like even more than centuries. All of the full magnitude of all of this, took only the ten hours that he slept.

He would thus see Brahimian, Celestial, Nomiruan and Human history into the past, present and future. It would take him one full moon cycle, to vacate the total thrall of all of this and return to something more similar to his usual state, but he was changed forever!

He had visited the places of life, for all the people's ancestry, of all who were close to him now. After the festival of his return, the Brahim would touch him and say, Amayn, or in English, Amen. And everyone wanted to touch and be touched by the sacrament of his journey.

Here was a bed of riches glowing in the life-stream of living waters. Here on the streams bed of sand and pebbles, lay glowing, vast treasures. Treasures of peoplehood. All his lineage included all the lineage of the ones, who touched him, even distantly, as trees reaching out to other trees and thus to all, in the fullness.

He had peered into every soul, that his soul emanated from, including our Maker. Couples that conceived their children, together with God's involvement, whether they saw this or not. Every soul before Aundeiri, in every realm of time, had their place in his soul and they were all wondrous to him. Tears beyond joy filled him. He could never forget any part.

Man is meant to meet God every day, and so we all make room for the One who always makes room for us. Not by praying, but by living, in a way, where there is no distance, between ourselves and our Source. The day itself becomes a prayer.

Without want and graced with plenty, thought of owning does not arise, only scarcity breeds this. Where scarcity cannot be found, the living will love to give gratefully. To be gracious to another, each soul finds a momentary home, where none are strangers, but friends.

Chapter Thirteen
How Far?

Such were the journeys of the soul. Some 'day' nothing would be hidden. Ancestral time travel issued forth from it, how involved in every instant, Life Giver actually was, is, ever shall be. How He was the most vital part, in the make-up of our souls. We are a part of Him, as He is a part of us. Seeing that more clearly is central to the evolution of the soul. Life is nourished by truth. Life has a most powerful basis, that of where it comes from. That truth is where we rest in trust. He has never been hidden. Though once we hid from Him. As we evolve, we cease the hiding. For example, His miracles, we must feel them in order to see them! Until we trust, we cannot feel. Until we feel, we cannot see.

Having seen into the deepest regions of those souls in connection with Aundeiri gave him a clearer picture of Life Givers total connection with every soul that He crafted. With the depth of His love for them and commitment to them and the fulfillment of their lives as part of His own. An amazement at this total intimacy with every life as generated from our Makers love for His creation and the signal accomplishment of further perfection on all levels, by the further genesis of their every evolution.

It was here that Aundeiri began to see the children of Lurynda and himself. In the mirroring of all else that he had just seen. The families in creation by the single Hand. How nations as well are formed through this Divine planning. How Abrahamic families all, had derived from single root. By the name of Abraham. How it did not seem to Aundeiri, at this moment, that he could ever love them more. Yes, he would, just the same. He had gained the understanding that might help him to finish the third little book. How history was beginning to really shine for him.

They now had two daughters and three sons. They all could manifest hugely powerful wings and leap together as family, in wreath of realms flight. Leaping through the veil into the much beyond, consciousness. To places no ship could fly to. All seven of them flying in single consciousness as multiplied by the powers of each to make the whole. At first moments they seemed to themselves quite physical. They really did not know that a transcending phenomena, was taking place, over the place where these "rules" apply. So enthralled in their experience, that conjecture to analyze had no place at all for them. This root of Abraham, to open himself in God's guidance, without doubt or question, was still bearing fruitfulness and multiplying.

They would have many more children together and swarms of grandchildren. With lives exceeding one-hundred-twenty-thousand- of years, time, this was nearly unavoidable. To the rafters of any home, would well be filled with generations of fully adult offspring. Aundeiri's army.

Using the enormous transport ships of the past was still practiced, mostly to bring "Noah" cargoes teeming with plant and animal life from various billions of home worlds. Sometimes bringing settlers seeking total emersions of living off the land with and for their children. In the Earth time of 18756 AD, Aundeiri's vastly extended family now ran in the millions. It was said the new home world might be named Aundeiri and so with much protest from the man in question, the name was given.

Space, having become brighter by the light of our souls, brought us to a most distant land. Reflective moons bounced light back from generous suns at locations and gravities perfect for life. This was a place of rushing torrents of water and frequent electric storms, yielding ionic ozone transfer cleansing, as after a rain, alongside the crashing waves of clear waters and verdant, pastoral countryside. A monster of a star was this new Eden, so full of promise. The first home built was named the house of

Eleazar, in honor for a grand ancestor living at the cusp of the last dark age and in the first day of blessing to follow. Whom but Life Giver could have dreamed all of this?

The single, story house was of the ancient Nomiruan style as derived from ancient Japan. The inner dwelling portion spanned in excess of a city block, while the surrounding generous porches doubled that, yet again, with aisleways to more dwelling space adding on. Folks could live in great number in these homes. Often, small rivers meandered through the structures built to include them and with a central lake within, for public bathing. Since all the waters were flowing, they never grew stale. Fish abounded and all the toilet waters were carried by buried pipes to distant deep holding basins until they finished breaking into soil once more. Many of these homes had inner open areas, so as to never feel enclosed, but elevated by the open skies. Vaulted cielings for fifteen footers.

Man is meant to meet God every day, and so we all make room for the One who always makes room for us. Not by praying, but by living, in a way, where there is no distance, between ourselves and our Source. The day itself becomes a prayer. With Redwood trees reaching for the light, standing four times taller than on Earth. Oceans of clear water as vast as anywhere. Sea going fish, good to eat and weighing in as palatable monsters. What a paradise for horses and children. Without want and graced with plenty, thought of owning does not arise, only scarcity breeds this. Where scarcity cannot be found, the living will love to give gratefully. To be gracious to another, each soul finds a momentary home, where none are strangers, but friends.

Grand wooden sailing ships upon the waters, to live exploring. Each day to find a new world. With distances that call for vessels on a grand scale, to adventure in the thousands. Guitars the size of cellos, to deliver deep rumbling Spanish passions. To sing completely free. This Megastar would take centuries to explore.

The Eternal chose Jerusalem to manifest His Son as Messiah. From whose Hand, all creation was and is, enacted. By His Father's will and desire, in all existence. For all time, the Son has enacted, by His Father's will. The disclosure of the Son made manifest in Jerusalem. The Hand of Creation, Messiah, was to be seen in Jerusalem.

History is a story of past eternity, of present eternity, of which the future is a continuance. Messiah, the Spirit Warrior, King of Jerusalem, returned to the Father, all that was lost, during the Tribulation. His people sought a place of safety, to return to Jerusalem, their God given home. To live in peace, at last. Messiah delivered this justice.

Chapter Fourteen
Horizonal Shift

N o matter how far we may travel, the core, unifying, reality is there. The Perfect Unity, within all creation. Touching this, fear and pain vanish. This time out, reports were coming in, that fewer stars and planets were found. Could there be an end? Or is the expansion such that great distances from anything, is mathematically normal and equivalent?

A time of reflection, taking in all that had occurred, helped us to settle in. We, as a single, filled by many. As it was said, on ancient Earth, "Out of many, one." The mad dash, of exploration, was now more even keeled and steady.

Space was becoming more luminous, even in areas without suns and stars producing light. Was it coming from our souls? Almost as if the interior light of creation, was becoming progressively exterior. We were developing an evolutionary shift, that required ever less physical brightness to see.

It seemed, at least in part, that our souls were illuminating wherever we traveled. While space was expanding so fast, that fewer planets and stars, were revealed. Longer journeys between encounters.

It also felt like we were merging with the Divine Intelligence. Without need of giving up our physical bodies. Maybe we would get to a point where physical and nonphysical eternality, separate and distinct, could be completely equal, with God in the middle. Was this the journey Life Giver was taking us on? Where out there and in there, were one? An horizontal, paradigm shift, occurring within our evolution. Timeless, limitless, oneness.

"Behold, Israel, the Lord is God, the LORD is ONE." Truth and the hope, that it inspires, spring eternal, setting us free from any form of bondage and returning us into the arms of our Maker. The largest gathering ever, called to take place, on the thirty-six planets of Zan, was to be a plenum, to focus on whatever we might find together, hand in hand, circles widening, as an all soul's embrace. A rendezvous! No ships would be used, all were to come, through internal means and all could, as it turned out. Representatives from everywhere were arriving, including millions of species that no one had ever physically "seen" before.

The planets of Zan had God's Touch places, all the way to the surface and all the way through. A tuning fork, for discovery. The thirty-six, had healing properties throughout their entirety: soil, water, air, and so in every food as well. They would be joined in the great honesty, Life Giver presiding. Completely formless and any other form. Some intelligent entities did not need bodies at all.

Earth's contingent was quite the surprise. By their ancient measure of time, it would be 7008 AD. They were changed, most of all. Physical and nonphysical living beings gathered to make a reckoning of newly discovered realities. Angels could be killed, like those long ago, who defied God life and freedom. They were conditionally immortal, just so long as they were good. They could be killed, like Satan and his fallen angels were.

All living beings were capable of immortality, by living in alignment with the Ultimate Unity. Eternal life reckoned by the Sword of Truth. Gifted to them by the Lord God's Hand. Those who truly lived and died were resurrected, in the delight of the Living Creator, whose aliveness was transmitted into them, and then they rose. These ultimate realities had never been about religion. They were reality. What is. Knowing God, shall we not do well?

The resurrected were forever alive, by the path they chose,

by their own will. With whatever gifting they might receive, the result of immeasurable generosity. From the Living Aliveness. So many species nearing perfection. To include Earthlings, once believed to be of the least intelligence, until most died, all the worst of them. They accelerated their evolution from there, in an almost straight up trajectory. The seed was within them. The Nomiruan were proof. Only the One, was both all physical and nonphysical, the bridge between all dimensions.

Jake and Ari were laughing together. Anciently, there were those who would always invite the Presence to enter into them and join with them. In contrast, were those practicing ceremony by rote, without contact, spewing doctrine and liturgy, without spiritual aliveness. Rabbi Ari lev, Lion Heart, once mentioned to Jake, how few in the clergy, actually believed in God and how show business had taken over. This truth had lain upon him, painfully, for an infinity! Living his life in connection with the One of All.

With ecstatic visions and voices. With revelatory encounters. In the heart of natural reality. Symptoms of healthy and normal psycho-spiritual function. Animated by more than just physical perception. Visionary communion is the natural state, of those loving their creator. Ancient Judaism and Christianity both, were experiential practices. They lived their days in focus, toward encountering the Living God. But then Rome introduced a power struggle between religion and experience, to kill the latter, to get more power, taken from God, given to the claws of Empire.

"Do you remember what I told you so long ago? That you must oppose evil with all the force within you, by the Hand of Ha Shem? How this must include the violence necessary to liberate the oppressed, and deliver justice for them, by the Name of Hashem? How this is the work of a true servant of the Living God? For there are times when all levels of warriorship are required. So, my brother, do not hate the sword, but love those who need your help.

"Look at what Human Beings have become. They are way beyond us, without even being resurrected. Ha Shem has blessed more than we might have imagined. Each generation has found their key to Eternity, by opening their hearts and inviting the heavens into them.

"The concept of shituff, before Messiah, was to ride, touching the prayer shawls, of the righteous, into the Kingdom of the Heavens. Then, with Messiah, all could touch the Life Key and be filled with the Sacred Presence.

"Immediately, Satan offered an alternative path. The seemingly, loving nurturance, of the serpent. Offering a way around the Eternal Gift, made to appear even brighter in appeal, than the path of life. To seduce the unwary, pretending truth.

"While that seduction was bringing in its first fruits, the next stage was to enter into the church with demonic possession. Then the demonic church entered politics. Mass murder under the banner of religion. Now the false church-state, could make a 'holy campaign,' against the faithful Jews and Christians, hunted down for 'righteous' sport. A necessary consolidation of their power.

"All species are holding hands now, to enter together, the ecstatic seizures of revelation. To see as one. You were kept alive through the narrowest of death experiences, to help you pass through the veil, into the whole. Then you asked for the protection of your community, which they received, given to all those within this circle.

"Long before that, your services as warrior, became that of teacher. Teacher means Rabbi. That has always been the job you were called to do. Lacking recognition of that by others, meant nothing. They were jealously unfit to judge you. That discomfort humbled you, only making you better. For a while, the peace was too quiet for you. Then you opened your heart more than ever, to receive your next command, 'Live beyond conflict, as all must learn to do,' and now you teach infants, with vast intelligence streaming from their eyes. They are different than your Hebrew school students, that you taught so long ago. As before, you continue to teach, in whole simplicity, what the interior light can do.

"These tiny young children, see so clearly, what you had to struggle life long, to catch just a glimmer of. They love you as a fellow infant. They appreciate your simplicity, your desire to serve humbly. Your soul is sweet to them. But you are like a pet. A noble, magnificent, beast to them."

Laughing, "You describe it well. My intelligence grows slowly within me, by the Eternal Light. While serving rooms full of genius babies, so far beyond any concept of genius my mind could conjure.

"We are worthy ancients, who breached the walls, to provide justice, on behalf of children and mothers, we cannot begin to fathom. We have truly earned our humility. To be seen as the ancient warriors, of those primitive times, fighting those goblins of the past, where evil had been permitted to rise. We are like prehistoric creatures, with little brains and big hearts, fighting for freedoms, that may now be taken as given circumstance. And we used to think ourselves intelligent!"

With big laughter, Jake's old Rabbi said, "We don't even know what intelligence might look like. But we are the foundation stones of a mighty future. The Jewish and Christian journey has led us all here. The Law, as written down by Moses, has informed all law, into the present. Mitigated only by what this sustenance of law looks like, as it is now, no longer challenged by an evil impulse. Sometimes these subtleties have a high order of magnitude over time. Therefore, we say, 'Hear, oh Israel, the Lord Imminent is also Absolute Creator, The Lord is ONE.' The One giving the wholeness of peace."

Then, as if these words had called it in, came the sweeping change, like a tsunami. When all species drew together in circles, holding hands, suddenly the huge God's Touch, brilliant colors and energies, surrounded us.

But then, an even more spectacular event took place, on all planets everywhere together. The fiery, electric coppers, golds, silvers, yellows and oranges of God's Touch outpouring were then enveloped in an even brighter barrage of opalescent silvers, molten electric fiery whites and many shining neon purples. These two phenomenal giftings, caused us all to glow luminously, with an amazement of light. Uplifting energies bringing us to euphoric heights none might dream of. Lifted while our feet remained grounded. We were beginning to see all the undiscovered places, both with many as yet to be created, along with those not yet found. This was prophesy, being shared with all that lives. Life is the most powerful force, other than Life Giver Himself, the giver of all life, designed to be free. Freedom is the most powerful attribute of life.

After all of this swept through us, we remained still, while an infinity of awe, held our focus. Every planet and star, with every living soul, sang a melody that was transmitted into all existence. Bringing a family like togetherness. An explosive increase. Nobody had the desire to make words, but rather nonverbally, we began to prepare a festival. A richness for all tastes. We would never be the same. Our hearts were full.

Joyous tears without words. Nothing adequate could be said. An evolution for us all. Euphoric, nearly painful, heart-bursting love. Our encampments would stay together for many orbits. Bathed in the inexpressible. Then came the Voice.

"Speaking especially to those of you, who lived through the terrible past. I inspired you, every time I made an intervention on your behalf. Those of you who saw that, surely knew I had My Hand upon you. As children you felt this whenever you needed rescue. You beheld the miraculous as normal. When you were unsafe you felt protected. That you were never alone. When you cried out, I was there, with you. I knew who or what was coming after you, when My intervention saved you. I felt your complete trust. Now teach My history."

Physical space travel saw a major decrease. New as yet unvisited places were instead visited by telepathic, remote viewing. Having already seen them, through the Gathering, the great visitation, that gave the natures and locations into perpetuity. Deep dreamers could now open the gates, to enter the communion of the whole.

This was a dimension of pivotal change. The telepathic web saw entry, at greater depth, in the interior of audio-visual contact, engaging all known senses. Web-streams finding an intensity of intimacy. Strangers taking to each other as family. Lessening the distance between physical and nonphysical, social reverie. Closing trans-personal separation. To begin a revolution of intimacy.

A rising intimacy, making us as one. That led to teleporting for physical presence, amid the growing multi-magnitude of close friends. Fostering mass migrations, compelled toward proximity and to enable studies of home worlds. These were fine adventures, as the result of resettlement.

The Telon, those of the Inner Wing, were quite tall, thin and graceful, with a broad wingspan. Bird like feet and without hands. They could hover above ground as long as they desired. The absence of hands made it necessary to move tools by mental control, telekinesis. They built entire cities and technologies, by developing mind manipulation to build intricate devices or other wonders, by the hand of the mind. Writing books, songs and blueprints as well as painting or whatever. Intelligence had cleared the way, to invent and construct. During the Thousand, their constructs made formidable weaponry, that few could resist or defend against, making for a thrifty and effective war fighting. Thereby exacting, in gravest consequence, victories against the ravening hordes of evil, death dealers.

Their wings were multi-folded wonders of strength and endurance. They had long legs, clawed feet, long necks and penetrating eyes. One of the Telonian Priests said to Flux, the Nomiruan Priest, "We have mutual connection with the Messiah, who is partly of Human and thus Nomiruan heritage. Our minds developed advanced telekinesis long ago, only to see deeply into the past, present and future. We were actually watching the passionate sacrifice, during His mission, to touch Humanity forever. We share in your spiritual roots most deeply, by direct experience of Messiah. We began physically but invisibly, visiting the Jewish people throughout their history, as the result of our love for them. Throughout Eternity, all the multiverse, revolves around Jerusalem."

Flux, "The Eternal chose Jerusalem to manifest His Son as Messiah. From whose Hand, all creation was and is, enacted. By His Father's will and desire, in all existence. For all time, the Son has enacted, by His Father's will. The disclosure of the Son made manifest in Jerusalem. The Hand of Creation, Messiah, was to be seen in Jerusalem."

Another Telonian Priest, "By passing through me, Life Giver can transmit to another. By looking up with an open, empty vessel, filling with the energies being sent to her. An empty cup, then filled with spirit and the water of life, for her to drink. A priestly function, discreetly accomplished, with a servant's humility. We, the humble, inherit the Sacred Wind, in this way."

Flux, "History is a story of past eternity, of present eternity, of which the future is a continuance. Messiah, the Spirit Warrior, King of Jerusalem, returned to the Father, all that was lost, during the Tribulation. His people sought a place of safety, to return to Jerusalem, their God given home. To live in peace, at last. Messiah delivered this justice."

Yet another Telonian Priest, "In the worst of the Tribulation, the Abomination of Desolation, was for Jerusalem, a two-tiered terror. Germanys,' Holy Roman Empire, encamped all over the

City of Peace, while the Satanic antichrist stood in hatred, upon the Temple Mount. At the end of it, the people rejoiced, in the city of God's rescue. The dwelling place of peace. The Gihon Spring now flows within the walls of the Millennial Temple, under its altar. The world revolves around Jerusalem, as does the multiverse."

Mind and soul, travel, accomplishes extensive communication. All senses are connected. Even those we cannot name. Still, teleporting vast distances, through total telekinesis, provides adventures for families and educational junkets. Spacecraft are used for resettlement. Along with herds of wildlife shuttling with them.

An entire universe within every living being is met by a multiverse in dynamic expansion. Physical advancements pale before the rising tides of realization. In various dimensions, travel is a constant. The definition of reality expanding continuously. An open ended, thrall and thrill, with a celestial rhythm reaching ever outward. Intelligence grows to perceive it, otherwise to be overwhelmed entirely. Intelligence is a trait of aliveness and life is an unlimited trait, in its very nature.

Evolution is unassailable, while the genesis   of creation, emanates from the ultimate, organizing intelligence. Because it is a mathematical impossibility, for all life and existence to be a mere, accidental, litany of events.

Evolution is a fundamental attribute of creation!

Chapter Fifteen
Spirit Warriors

There is no single infinity code or immortality key. There are as many of these as there were, are or will be, living souls. As many as there are, resurrected. Each of us will be examined to receive, each of our destinations. No single heaven, but as many as are needed. We all find our way home in our own way." Naomi taught so clearly. Sam replied, "One Creator with His Son and Sacred Wind, in unity, making One. With as many names as voices that have been lifted up calling out to Him. Physical longevity can also be unending.

"What is infinite, is the number of souls, living in connection. The number of souls fastened in their living connection and by their actions taken in this alignment. Leading to immortality. The only key, or code, is the sacred road, with infinite tributaries, all that lead home. For all of us. Our joy is in these life roads."

Naomi, "The infinite number of genetic possibilities, make for a vastness of differences in life forms. There are a few qualities, that are present in all life. The need to feed, reproduce and evolve. Adaptability is the precursor to evolution, without which survival is threatened. All life needs a flowing, energy source, like a sun. Life requires water to dissolve nutrients and chemicals. If you want to find life, follow the flow of water and energy. The more energy utilized, the greater evolvement, of the species."

Sam, "Lastly, there is the great need, for intelligent life, to touch and be touched, by the creative forces. By the Ultimate Source, behind the genesis, of all creation. As the dynamic flowing of life force, in all life, is certainly proof, that life itself, is the core energy, that everything else is flowing from."

Now, a number of Telonian Priests, joined in the exchange. "Most of our priesthood are avid scientists as well. Adaptations, bringing positive mutations, are the change needed, on the path of creating through evolution. We Telon had to devise, the means, to make our brains provide the hands, we were not born with."

"Telekinesis was then our top priority. Downstream in time, long ago, we began our visits to other home worlds. We were to accelerate our development, as learning brought us along. Necessity nurtures invention, making a weakness, the father of creative evolution. So that greater treasure, might be found."

"On various home worlds like Earth, anciently, it was once thought that science and spirituality, contradicted one another, becoming mutually exclusive, between each other. Our abilities to explore for reality, have shown us, that the two are complimentary and supportive of one another. The seven days of creation were not meant, necessarily, to be literal days, but periods of time."

"Evolution is unassailable, while the genesis of creation, emanates from the ultimate, organizing intelligence. Because it is a mathematical impossibility, for all life and existence to be a mere, accidental, litany of events. Evolution is a fundamental attribute of creation!"

"We have heard the song of life, in our spiritual communions and in our scientific discoveries. The deeper we go into science, the more we see of the miraculous nature, of the creative presence, of our Life Giver. Life force is the predominate energy of creation! Therefore, the what is, of science, dances together, with the what is, of the spirit. Together, the two, are one, in the unity of existence.

Humanity, anciently, had held itself back, under the constant siege of Satanic influence. After removing that besiegement, they rapidly came into being, what they had been designed to be.

Sensing and feeling empathically, opens the door to intuition. Infusing into those who are open. With more opening, comes telepathy. Then the door is pried further, enabling teleportation, through vast regions of space, times and dimensions.

Chapter Sixteen
Dawn Of The Celestials

I keep falling in love with every breath and seeing more of you, each moment passing. Our children conceived in fusion, with our Maker and ourselves. Three loves uniting, for the creation of a child, filled with the resonance, of three souls and united, finally, into the fourth soul, the one that soars."

They knew that prayer before sex, could stir the celestials, engaging the song of creation, to rise up to a brilliant dawn. Inviting the Living Presence to bless and endow their child with more even, than they could dream to ask for, so as to place the creation of their new child, in divine hands. For blessed reproduction.

Their glistening skin was moist to the touch and a symphony of pastels. Large eyes of gray shades, shaped as almonds, broadly set apart, having a depth that suited their intensity. Ten or so feet tall, swiftly they ran. The world they knew was alive from the inside out. They saw how Life Spirit spoke through nature in the world they were rooted to.

They had always been telepathic, but preferred to sing to one another, from loving hearts. Their music was passionate and fierce. Arising from the deep well of life force and strength. Resolute, deliberate, in a recently created Edenic world with deserts, jungles and fertile plains. At night, the luminescent expanse, densely populated with flora and fauna, teeming wildlife appearing somehow bigger than life.

Uninterested in time travel, the web, or visiting other worlds. Way too much in the here and now, to break deep focus, in what held fascination for them. Super intelligent, while living in child like wonder. They found, in their lives, all they would ever need. They, and their world, were alive, with their field of dreams, directly under their firmly planted feet. Yes, they were powerful.

The pan-species trend toward staying on home world, was another evolutionary leap. An, phenomena of awareness. All the knowledge and experience on the web, had been seeping into the Cosmos, emanating into all that lives. Every vessel able to contain it, could reach for the low hanging fruit. A profound evolution in awareness and common ground for all to walk upon.

The Free Ones, as they called themselves, were unconcerned with the endless expanse, having already an overflowing cup. Born with abundant life from within, feeling deeply that every need was in their hands. No calling out, to reach out for, Life Spirit or other beings, as the conversation was already intimate. Right there within them, emanating from the inside dwelling place of their world and the ground they stood upon. The skies too, were reaching down to embrace them. Living the Kingdom of Heaven, from within themselves.

They were given true paradise. They lived in the huge trees everywhere. In natural harmony. For them, there was nothing that was not alive. Nothing that was not sacred. They only craved privacy when it came time to make love and procreate. This was most sacred, the inner sanctum, where they were joined with Life Spirit, to make a child. To gift their child, into his soul, through the transmission, of the three progenitors. Taking deliberate responsibility for what their child would be born to be.

The time was 8953 AD, planets and stars were now just called worlds, calling in more relevant qualitative natures, to best describe them. Dimensions are also worlds and they too, are infinite. Dimensionally, every world in turn, can be yet another infinity, of numberless, timeless, endless expanse.

Ancient conceptions were peculiar. To think evolution would breed physical weakness for example. It was nonsense that evolutionary change would produce weaker bodies with huge brains. Physically and mentally, it is strength that increases survivability. Both Human and Nomiruan, having come to a point similar to that of the Free Ones. Evolution spurs survivability, thus adapting for relevant change, in a slingshot dynamic of change. Stronger minds with stronger bodies and souls.

Humanity, anciently, had held itself back, under the constant siege of Satanic influence. After removing that besiegement, they rapidly came into being, what they had been designed to be. Accelerated evolvement was making them indistinguishable from their Nomiruan paradigm. They both sped together, into dramatically faster evolution, having pulled out the stops on their genetic trail. A release, of oppressive tension, sent them forward together, toward their potential.

Human growth had been stunted, under the mass hypnosis of evil and so their explosive development, when mixed, by interbreeding, caused a radical genetic launching, for both species. This is how the spiritual can interact with physical forces for the betterment of all. The Free Ones saw them as kindred spirits and developed an affectionate and strong rapport with them. They would run together, spontaneously, dance and sing and the spirit rose so all could hear, the song of creation, living in them. All three species were about ten feet tall and tremendously powerful.

Sensing and feeling empathically, opens the door to intuition. Infusing into those who are open. With more opening, comes telepathy. Then the door is pried further, enabling teleportation, through vast regions of space, times and dimensions. The web allows for the most intimate, nonphysical encounters. Lifting the veil, to all soul's entry. Our tiny infants are open to the endless expanse in all dimensions. The web of nonphysical exchange, and its counterpart, in physical exchange. When joining the two together, the doors swing wide open, to provide potentially limitless travel. A telepathically web informed, telekinesis, and teleportation. The engine for it all, is the soul.

Merging with the endless expanse, into consciousness, reaching inward, to every soul. Our interior vessels, emptying, opening, as we made a unified effort to endow ourselves, with an adequate vessel to receive it all. A knowing, our inner expanse, embraced the total expanse. Synchronicity, an infinity of all dimensions, held together in experience. Another leap into realization.

The Free Ones, along with the Human-Nomiruan, now a single species, were an adventuresome bunch. With uninhabited worlds, an endless number of them, far outnumbering those inhabited. Calling Jonan, of the Free Ones, to suggest to Hariru, of the Hunomiruan, as they were now named, "Hey Bub, listen up now.

"Why not get the largest transport ship and fill it, like Noah's Ark, with the most amazing critters, from among all that have been found. Also, fish and seeds of all kinds, for a plenitude, upon new ground."

Ru, "It's all been done before, so why now, yet again? As a pilot program, leading toward populating all worlds? I love this Jo and I'm all in, when do we get started?"

Jo, "It's like this, Mr. Ru, how about yesterday? Now that the Kiger Horse has been selectively bred for size, along with the Buffalo and so many others, we should tear into this now."

Ru, "Since we give ourselves permission, the time to take action is now. We begin staging here, while we call out for help in selecting and shipping our lists from the home worlds where they are most plentiful. Thought should be given, about starting these populations without predators at first. So that we can establish populations before putting them at risk. Too much of anything, then needs predation, to keep balance."

Every sort of life was streaming in. Along with every sort of fodder, to emplace within the Ark. This was true adventure and sentient beings, of all sorts, were streaming in with them. Some to facilitate, others with the view to resettle with them and watch over them, upon new ground.

The world they picked was enchanting and as yet unnamed. With more gravity here, larger animals would thrive over smaller ones. Three suns illumined this enormous world, whose constant, explosive, eruptions, scattered electromagnetic showers, producing widely different and magnificent light shows. It was hard not too slow down and just watch it all. Trees much taller than skyscrapers and with so large a base diameter, twice that of a city block. Entire colonies or villages or tribes, could easily be housed in one. Jo raised his deep tremolo voice, to carry his joyful outburst, "The Free dwell in the tree, how about thee?"

Ru issued a rousing soliloquy, "Once kicked out of Eden, Adam and Eve had to toil by the sweat of their brow. But that was very long ago. Now, the abundance of everything, sets all Life Giver's children, off to loftier pursuits. We only have to identify our desires and off we go. We live free of material needs, giving us the means to design our destinies, without the interference of scratching out a living day to day. Life Spirit has always created out of His desire and His intention is that we do the same. Spontaneous movements and changes, just springing up from the delight of our desire and from the purpose of that desire. Unbounded creativity springing forth, calling us to put the finishing touches on perfection. We are creating, as the means, for Life Giver to perfect us."

Jo, "Thus our strong desire to attain to a perfect, primal state and live as the wild creatures live. Adding on only what might be desired. Farming, fishing, swimming, hunting, riding, flying, just living, in perfect freedom. In alignment with all that is life. Yes, we bring our musical instruments or make them as we do our bows and arrows."

Ru, "Raising our families in the wild, before bringing them

toward other pursuits. So that they will always return to that primal freedom, for the sake of their children. Grounded in life as natural beings. The natural world sustains the soul, by keeping us in connection. Sleeping in trees or in the open, waking up in wonder. Ready to launch the next adventure of every living day passing. Teaching us always, to begin again daily, in deep reverence toward life and freedom and the One giving life to us all, each day passing."

Kadir, of the Eritry, "Just as the Disunited States of America, triggered the 'Great Tribulation,' our spiritual unity with all that is, provides us with serene unity. Which equals working together, across all dimensions. By reaching out to Life Giver, who then reaches back. This reality of connection, has always brought in the wholeness of peace."

Flux, of the Hunomiruan, "Our latest Ark Project, has been joined by countless souls. Earth's Aurora Borealis, is caused by the way the sun's energies are refracted, by the orbits of Earth. Here we have three Suns, with similar phenomena, doing this, with eight Moons, adjusting for gravitational integrity, holding orbits on track. Every world needs the right gravity, source of light or heat and liquid water, to generate life. When I look at phenomena like this, on planet Eden, these constant showers of energy, propelling all these fantastic, celestial, caresses of light and color, render me speechless. We have become Edenites, all!"

Ardor of the Howan, "Our new, wild, paradise, filling, with every wondrous creature, abounding. Soon to be teeming with life of every kind. Like the peacock looking, giant flyers, with high enough intelligence to make it hard to classify. They totally love to take other living beings for a ride to anywhere. Telepathic animals. Or the galloping, rainbow colored, monsters that seem a little like a cross between a giraffe and an elephant, that also truly love to serve others. Such bright colorings and plumages of myriad creatures, nearly to rival the colors showering out of the skies. Yes, we will dress this new garden and keep it well, we shall ever do so. The challenge of matching creatures to environs and habitations, is another aspect of walking with Creator, to finish creation."

He then began ecstatic weeping, overwhelmed by trying to describe all that he was seeing. Also, the tremendous variety of sentient beings, that came to join and participate in this noble venture. Truly a wonder as well.

The vast trees, had little tree houses, built into the trees themselves, whose bark alone, measured roughly twelve feet deep. A multitude of wild creatures were dwelling in harmony with all the sentient beings. Trees becoming as populous as villages or small towns. Although many species cared to live among their own kind, more did not. Living together, all together, in primal state, was yet another evolutionary leap in behavior. Adapting together, while living in wild circumstance. The organizing force behind all of this was Divine, the living paradigm!

They were in the business of love. To hold and be held. To snuggle up with animals, or sentient beings. They were like an animal themselves, instinctively feeling who the other was, much like the Kiger Horse do.

They looked like animals. Aside from their formidable powers, they were animals, just smarter than almost anyone. They rode upon the shoulders, of mighty warriors, who became like children, at play, with these amazing, tiny, creatures... these five-pound marvels of creation.

Chapter Seventeen
Looking Ahead, The Deep Dreamers

The deep dreamers of tomorrow, were conceived, surrounded, in the Light of Creation. These conceptions were guided ones. Asking for Divinely inspired infants and receiving them. The family, still at the nexus of life. New life as the building blocks of the future. Sacred procreation is where man meets Creator. Most species, practiced this, to reach higher and deeper, into an illustrious future. To conceive with resolute purpose. Making for better fruit on the tree of life.

Trust is the most powerful prayer, although wordless, Life Giver hears our silent prayer, completely. Then we are held in His trust. Feeling the energy flow from the interior light of creation, as it fills our life force. Luminous energy flowing with our alignment, Sacred Wind blowing through us and bringing us to life. Trust is the most valuable commodity, in relationship with each other.

Lifting focus here, toward how we lived. A familial bond between the Free Ones, the Hunomiruan and Howan, was growing in the trees of Eden. Very physically adept climbers all, scampering about in blissful, primal living. Extremely powerful while always seeking to live in simplicity. Their prowess suited them to being amazing warriors, who have no war to fight. Making love with life, in harmony and peace. Tender hearted and truly loving. No matter how tough they might appear.

All of them ten feet tall and athletic. With lifespans over one hundred thousand years. At the moment of death, they shed their physical bodies to attire themselves with spiritual ones. Spontaneous change in seamless transition. All beings today in 11096 AD, lived between the material and spiritual, the two sides of life, so intimately that dimensional shifting had mostly been done already. Death had been receding from the shores of living waters. For tens of millennia.

There was no role to play, for death. Without evil, death has no purpose. Death had been on trial for irrelevancy. When would death time out? Death was transcended. Those sheltering under the wings of Life Giver had always transcended death. Such remote, distances of time, had been spanned always, by those at war with evil!

This was true for the Angelic hosts as well. Concealed with the resurrected until the end of the Great Tribulation. That time when the Divine pleaded with Humankind, through destruction. Had they turned back to Him, the time of troubles, could have easily been cancelled. Since they were unreachable, He plowed into them, for the sake of the true, who became targeted by Satan, for the ultimate holocaust. Against those who dared to follow the sacred path: the, Song of Names, God's names. Singing of the names, of the many Divine attributes, of the Intimate Absolute. On the shores of Eternity, Singing the Song of Life.

Back to Eden. Their eyes would blink, and then viscous membranes would also blink, along with their outer eyelids. They were little and looked like the marsupials that dwelled in jungles. They had strong, retractable claws, but no ability to do what hands can do. They appeared to be small, insignificant animals. But when they blinked, they could command a supreme, visionary phenomena. While their outer eyelids were open, their blinking, inner eyelids, could shift about, for whatever level of seeing might be needed. In this manner, their eyes possessed a multitude of the ways of seeing.

When their cerulean blue eyes were activated, they viewed rather well, both in the physical and spiritual at once. With spectacular mind-soul reading. When their eyes were neon orange, they had telescopic and microscopic vision. To even see clearly, distant planets, or see through planets or other obstacles, to see beyond. When their silver purple eyes were on, they could peer deeply into the soul, with profoundly deep microscopic visioning. All three were counter transitional, coordinated to act as a singular inter-operational whole. They had no verbal speech. Yet their telepathy, vast and intricate. No one would have looked twice at them, at distance. But when they climbed up into the trees, no one nearby, could fail to see and feel, their intense power. For millennia they had cohabited with those having tactile hands. Inventors without peer or parallel. Affectionately snuggling with other beings. As they were evolving, it was their visionary talents that kept them alive. They could show up anywhere. These inconspicuous little savants were in fact, the very first beings to have ever done so. They never had the need to develop technology. They shared their inventions, with any who were capable of making use of them. They rode contently on the shoulders of the Free Ones, the Howan and the Hunomiruan. Who could then see as did the Amvry. In an expansively shared experience. Providing an elucidation for those blessed to have them around. There were never enough of them to go around, it seemed, until going still first, and asking for their assistance, while searching for unparalleled journey. They could augment perception in anyone, including animals, bringing everything together. In their way, they were mightier than those they rode upon.

Fortunately, there were billions of them to go around, on the soil of any world. With telepathy at the far reaches, and no spoken word, they had no names per se. Instead, their names were the sounds of a musical nature. These names were a symphony of ecstatic sounds, thrilling the soul to hear. Especially for the Howan, who became so joyous that they literally had to dance with the music.

The name Amvry, means The Hidden. Open all the while, in the extreme. Yet still, hidden. They were in the business of love. To hold and be held. To snuggle up with animals, or sentient beings. They were like an animal themselves, instinctively feeling who the other was, much like the Kiger Horse do. They looked like animals. Aside from their formidable powers, they were animals, just smarter than almost anyone. They rode upon the shoulders, of mighty warriors, who became like children, at play, with these amazing, tiny, creatures. These five-pound marvels of creation.

The Priest prays for others. To be discreetly their advocate. A Prophet listens until he hears God's message. To be discreetly, Heaven's advocate. By conveying to others, The Message. They are both to get out of the way! To discreetly vanish. Leaving those that were served, to be with Life Giver directly. Just to give the introductions while leaving. This process is also for Healers. To put God's Hand upon them. This is the way. This is the work.

Chapter Eighteen
Awarn's Bowl

The multiverse dwells within us. We dwell within each other. Our love touches all. We reach out to all. We reach in for family. For the intimacy of family. Love is Life Giver's reason for creation. He has been verbing us into existence. By the impetus of His boundless love. We do the same. It is by love that we create. All creation is carried on the rivers of love. As the Creator's image is reflected in His creation."

Awarn was an ancient, Priest, of Nomiruan descent. A Priest for all who enter the gates of rightful action. He had been pleading on behalf of trillions, across eons of time. Long before the Jerusalem of King David. Back to the times of Earth's creation. He knew many things. He was an ancient Teller who could bridge past and future. Even farther back, than Nomiru. Which had been similar to early Earth. A teacher to the quiet hidden ones. He had trained Flux from his childhood. He was a simple being, holding the bowl of complexities, over millions of years.

He was the last of the Ancients. From the Nomiruan mountain clan. Wearing black robes and those black diamonds, neon black! He liked to play with children. They were the best learners. His single simplicity was the result of his depth. He need only stand among others, to cause the Sacred Wind to pour through them and into others. No gathering was complete without him.

The earliest Nomiruan saw him as proof of God. He would say, "Look at the natural world as proof of God. Never me, our way is not one of sorcery. I am most truly, just one of you." Even the animals had reverence for him. But he turned away from power. Yet that only flowed more power into him. He knew full well of the dangers of power. Therefore, he tried never to display it. With utmost humility. This was how others felt his inner intimacy with life. His guiding influence gathered together, with single voice throughout time, all the children of life. He spoke about Messiah, Son of Life Giver, with tears in his eyes. He had known Him. Teaching from the Living Well. Yes, Awarn's bowl was always overflowing. At only five feet tall, lean and quiet, he looked more like a small Human, from prehistory. Life Giver commanded him to be a Priest only. To pray for others. In this, he had fought the accusations of Satan, launched against the innocent.

"The Priest prays for others. To be discreetly their advocate. A Prophet listens until he hears God's message. To be discreetly, Heaven's advocate. By conveying to others, The Message. They are both to get out of the way! To discreetly vanish. Leaving those that were served, to be with Life Giver directly. Just to give the introductions while leaving. This process is also for Healers. To put God's Hand upon them. This is the way. This is the work.

"Our job has been to walk in the way of Rabbi Jesus. Not just for Prophets, Healers and Priests. To make the introductions and then let others learn how to walk in these footprints. Teach them how to fish so they can go fishing. It is time to visit the Amvry on Eden. Those of the Mountain Guild, who are called, may join me. We will be there as long as it takes. We must learn their seeing. To call in, to our consciousness, what they can do. Merging with them to teach others, how to join with their consciousness. This melding has the potential to expand our depth. In order to better serve. They will be our teachers."

Once setting foot on land, dozens of the Amvry began leaping onto the shoulders of their new students. They had seen all of this in their deep dreams. They were excited and calling out in their high pitched, internal, voices, to announce that the spiritual luminaries of Nomiru had arrived. Flux ran to embrace Awarn. Reverberations of this joy were heard everywhere across the expanse.

The Amvry had an inner membrane, snakelike, over their

eyes. These viscous membranes began shuttering and thus shifting, to release their total vision. All the while, their outer eyelids would remain open. In review, cerulean blue opened the physical-nonphysical, to enhance the telepathy, throughout the range of extrasensory perception. Neon orange opened microscopic-telescopic visioning to see beyond. Silver purple opened deep, microscopic and telescopic visioning, to see deeply within. Each augmented the other way beyond any other psychic transfer. Guild members were now experiencing all of this, in an explosion of new seeing. Already they were being changed. Receiving a vast, megalithic inpouring of consciousness. A staggering load.

Flux to Awarn, "We must live and breathe together a very long duration. What You seek comes in slowly, like osmosis and continues to fill our cups, and faster, the longer we remain."

Awarn, "We are already beginning to stretch our vision mere moments after contact with these brilliant, tiny, creatures. Seismic expansion of our experiential reality. It is so strange that we only encounter them now. They certainly take their time."

Flux, "They have been content to influence in subtle ways, as they open dimensions in web exchange. Certainly, they have no shyness about them. The old adage may apply, that when the student is ready, the teacher will arrive."

They began sipping Nomiruan wine and the Amvry drank deeply, in their celebration of the next leap, as fostered by the habitations of Eden. Way up in the trees, we had small fire bowls that were used for cooking and warming. The night was young. The Amvry had never tasted Nomiuan wine before and although warned of its potency, they were getting tipsy. They were usually quite uninhibited. One goblet could inebriate several. So many trees full of five- pound wonders, filled with passionate emotions. They were now so friendly, and their telepathic music, inspirational, for all the tree dwellers.

Yes, they poured out their hearts. Soon, everyone was. A

more auspicious beginning could not be imagined. Deep friends overnight. Oaths were sworn, with great promise. We all had taken complete responsibility for the grand efforts being made. One promise, for the Amvry, was to live with all species as soon as practicable. The Web would soon be overflowing, just as the Amvry were, that special night.

During this historic, drunken spree, the Amvry laid themselves open, to be peered into. Hidden within their sleeping, subconscious minds, was the virtual treasure chest. The totality, of their experience, of reality. While the warrior species dreamt with them.

Everything Amvry, was passed between all who dwelled in those treas. Their tri-colored eyes were merely openings, to all that their souls could see. The Free Ones, Hunomiruan and Howan, slept and dreamt, snuggled up with the Amvry. The passing of spiritual seed. To impregnate future generations. All the beings in those trees, exchanged all that consisted of their identities. Regular telepathy went far. But hidden in the subconscious, lay the full magnitude, of all that their souls could see. Of the highest order, this was symbiosis complete. The vital transfer. Only through the vast rivers of identity exchange, could all the secrets, be fully seen. It was not the tri-color eyes, that gave sight, to the Amvry. That faculty was in their visionary soul, where the light of perception dwells. Eons before, their visionary eye capabilities, led them to evolve. To such an extent, that they developed, by evolution, such vision, that their triple eyes, were no longer needed. This hidden truth, of the Amvry, remained a secret, hidden from them, until the revelations, of the drunken spree. However, their consciousness was now evolving in tandem with all their new friends. Ripping through hyperspace, these revelatory awakenings brought the realizations forward, to be shared. "The Drunken Spree," brought deeper vision, at the Celestial Dawn level, for all to see. Yet another great festival, of that name, would be celebrated, by all that lives.

Amid the gatherings of Eden, were a multitude, of hitherto

unknown species. Revealed by the great gathering, taking place there. An astonishing, number of animals, were found to be both highly intelligent and sentient. The Amvry pointed out to the warrior species, all of these. Then, as transmitted to the Web, the Multiverse would be brought up to speed. The "Drunken Spree" festival, was now celebrated, by the massive drinking, of Nomiruan wine. The reward, for all this evolution, was to go out and get rip roaring drunk.

The Guild of the Mountain Clan, would stay on, living in the trees of Eden. A leap, of soul evolvement, had taken place. However, some things never change, like the need to get together and celebrate. These are times of intimacy. The next time Drunken Spree rolled around, for all celestials, dwelling anywhere, Awarn had something to say about it. "It will be high treason, if any of you are found, not properly drunk." Everyone yelled their approval!

One evening, as they sat together, at the community supper table, Awarn began to sing. "Dynamo of conviction. Path of purpose. Birth of rightful action. Here we stand together. Bridges to each other. Asking Life Giver's blessing. To rest in His hand. With faith like Abraham. Sweet comfort in our souls. As we rely on His guidance."

He often sang his blessings at the table, with words like these, before a meal. To him, everything, was a prayer. It was all Sacred. He was right. He was the most ancient Teller, that was still alive, in his physical body. Modest and discreet, ready for joy.

The primary result of evolution is joy. Over eons of time, he had seen brute primitives shedding blood. Now there was peace. He felt complete and whole. Joyfully holding children, he saw infinite promise. He was quite nimble for one some millions of years old. He remembered how primitive he had been and laughed softly.

Flux used to pick him up on his shoulders and run with him. A ten-foot Nomiruan, weighing in at three-hundred fifty pounds of muscle. A great warrior indeed. He was a soul warrior, just as were the entire mountain clan. Running with a one-hundred thirty-pound soul warrior, and a five-pound benefactor, riding along. Yes, Eden was full of miracles. Unfolding at such expansive speed that it seemed a microcosm of the endless expanse. To be sure, the leaps were revelatory in nature, for all in the Presence. These three were a powerful trio.

Waylon, the Scot, that got caught, in the light, "The Amvry have helped us open our circuits, to shine the light within. Opening circuits between us. Light opens the dark. Sharing the light, drives out the dark, where illuminations enable discovery.

"We teach beginners English with a new spin. Language using Me or I, lacks inclusivity and usually has a rude amount of ego. I feel, could be expressed as, we feel, the feeling is, or our feelings are. Male egotism is blurted out, female egotism is subtly contained. Anger tends to be an ego response and here, males and females, just blurt it all out. From their isolation, as polarized, by ego. Disconnection bares baleful results. How many fights could be avoided, using inclusive language?

"Almost all turmoil is aroused by ego driven self-importance. We drop ego to hear our creator or each other. 'Speaking for Myself, I refuse to hear you. I have things to tell you and you better listen.' Versus, 'Listen and hear, look and see, how brightly our future glistens.' Voices lifted in unison, for all we desire. We are not separate until we make ourselves so.

"Thus, the dawn of we the Living Celestials all, are ever clearing the path, to the revelatory, omni-present experience of all life. Seeing by the vision of an ongoing journey to the ultimate reality. Reality, the ever expanding, apprehension of it, delivers truth to the faithful. Our search is Life Giver's desire, that we move closer, so that He may move closer, to fill our cup. The energy of life pulsing throughout creation, is the inner voice causing us to sing the Song of Life. What is not Sacred?"

Benjamin, son of Jake, "Eden is spectacularly huge. With

trees of life everywhere. The place where we are invited to start over again, by the lights of every orbit. As new paradigm, for every newly discovered world, as yet unpopulated. The first Eden, of Adam and Eve, was where they were commanded to 'dress' the garden and name living creatures. These are the primal stories of new worlds. For those faithful, to finish creation. This of course, is service Multiverse wide. May the force of life be with us.

"Our sword is beyond praise, with any words, that are adequate. Designed for princely duties. Fashioned to slice through the darkness, with luminous awakening. It is the Sword of Truth, that delivers life. We are all distinct from one another. We all have our own path to walk. Yet when we draw together, to share the joy, we arouse inspiration and this praise, is adequate beyond any words."

As the advance of the infinite expanse was speeding up, the utter distance caused discovery of new worlds to slow down. Giving focus to inner expansion. Which equals faster individual growth.

Awarn, "Without fear, we are free. No matter our attainments, a child is still closer to God. A child may see Him face to face and live. Our spiritual intelligence might be considerable. Yet in the open simplicity of the child, He is able to reveal more. We have forgotten what we knew as children. The child may receive more than even Moses could. That is why Messiah said, 'Bring the children close to me. They are ready to receive. Such is the entry way to the Kingdom. In childlike simplicity."

Flux, "The Amvry have this kind of simplicity. Their children more so. Extra sensory perception and telepathy in particular, require simple openness to work. Before an Amvry child weighs one pound, they possess a level of connection with the Divine, that exceeds their parents. When they sing their names, those hearing them are brought to tears of recognition. Their profound union with life, in all its forces, is Sword of Truth deep."

That only by walking with Life Giver can we know reality. Only by His transmissions of light.

For all our discoveries, no matter how great, there is truly nothing but Life Giver. That is the how and the why, that the original Abraham, shows us the way of the living. The original plan, to bring us all together, all those that battled destructive forces through history.

Chapter Nineteen
Celestial Chariots

Some of them could hear Aether's voice. "Certain spectrum, of consciousness, are spiritual or material. Not limited by spacetime. Trans-dimensional spacetime folding, is an innate ability of those beings that have light in them. Once called astral travel, it is now well known, that it is about the interior light of being. Its energy manifesting throughout the infinite. Carried by luminous wings.

"Just as we love naming our children, all that we have cocreated, shine in much the same love. A creative frolic, in deep love. We are in love with our creation."

Not all of the newly discovered worlds were at all new. Not by any stretch. One in particular, may have been the most ancient of them all. The outer reaches of known space were outwardly so vast as to possibly contain any habitable world. Or so we speculated. Newly discovered worlds were rare indeed.

The oldest one had no interest in the Web. Or any encounter with other species. Save but two. They reached out to Awarn quite secretly, with a covert message to him. "Come see us. We are first creation. All Human, Nomiruan or Hunomiruan are invited. We have no interest in mass visitation. Please be supremely careful not to arouse any attention. Leave in small numbers, shifting under the veil of notice. We feel that you are finally ready to receive us."

Flux, Awarn and the most spiritually intelligent among the Mountain Clan, began arriving in trickles. First, they removed themselves, receding from proximity to others. Then, a few at a time, made the journey. To a place way beyond anywhere, that was known about.

God named them the Celestial, and their world, Heaven. Since the time of Abraham, the earliest Jews referred to the Heavens, in plural. These Heavens were known to be established by Life Giver. Wherever He chose. The seed, of Abraham, had been established on three worlds. Those faithful like Abraham. Transcending the great distances with a passion toward their Maker.

The Celestial greeted their fellow seedlings, with rare and intense love. They were of the spiritual family of Abrahamic faithfulness. Their cranium more capacious, by a half again. Greater in size and far more powerful. Their world was resplendent. These Celestial were a grand nobility. Could we really be of the same rootstock? Were we to become like them? We were stunned speechless, openly weeping. They were about thirteen feet tall. They made even Flux seem little.

A Celestial named David began embracing us with a love so nurturant that we began to tremble. He chided us gently. "How can you see Life Givers face and yet live? When you are overwhelmed, just to see your extended family. We are you. You are us. We dwell in a Heaven that is both material and spiritual." His eyes were the size of goose eggs. His power was like the resurrected Jake, who also was gently weeping. Moved deeply watching his kin meeting their future.

Sonegal continued, "To be cocreative, seeking the place where we may join in Divine Covenant, to conceive with Life Giver, in blessed exchange, making blessed babies. Just as we dress every newfound Garden of Eden, to put the finishing touches on creation. Beyond this, we cocreate with Life Giver, in blessed partnership. We Celestial dreamed to be doing more.

"As the Father told His Son, 'Make it so' whereby His Son created by His Father's Divine Word. Close to this, the Celestial coincide with Life Giver, in our song of life and thus we create, as God's little sons. Mirroring what the Son does. Life Giver began giving creative commands to certain of us. Covenant Creation by Life Giver's will, and our 'hand'"

The result of this higher level of co-creating was mind boggling to us. This humongous Star was more perfected than we had seen. Skies filled with mists and rainbows, in the ever falling, mists. Amid bright and clear skies, right down to the verdant ground, exploding with life.

The roaring rivers came from mighty springs and great lakes were all around the splendor. Yes, by the Hand of Life Giver, but also by the hands of His sons and daughters, that He so loved, living upon one of His favorite places. The Celestials creative hand, joined in all creation here, for eons. They were planning to bring, genetically, this level of being, to other worlds, wherever their Abrahamic relatives might dwell.

That now included an amazing number of worlds, both primal and "advanced." The three in one species, Human-Nomiruan-Celestial, were now making ready, to introduce new capabilities. Evolution was about to be kicked into hyperdrive! To the growing amazement of the two younger versions of the Celestial. Once, trillions of years ago, the Celestial were as primitive as the earliest Earthers.

They were made of the same genetic structure. All three could interbreed and conceive. On the evolutionary fast track, based upon the slingshot effect, coming from the Humans. Whose development had been retarded by satanic influence. Once relieved of that, the speed of change was an evolutionary accelerant for themselves and any choosing to interbreed with them. Thus, the last would overtake the first. Until they all were at levels beyond the current Celestial. An infinite expansion, genetically, lay in their future. Coming up quickly!

Hearing all of this, we were flat out dumbfounded. Speechlessly grasping for the clarity and the realization, that we were searching for. Looking around, these Celestial had actually dreamed up, most of what there was, in the enormity of this wonderful place. Plants, birds, fishes, animals, were all created by the Celestial, as guided by their Father.

Oldryn was much attracted to the elegant Zahnah. He was keen as a wolf, potentially a true super-warrior, but gentle as a dove. The first such cross, in the first week. The Covenant of marriage, consummating, under the Hand, of the One of All, who makes the bond.

She was a Priestess of the Mountain Clan Guild. Dressed in flowing black and with a necklace of the black diamonds of Nomiru. Quite tall, at nine feet. Brown hair and deep green eyes. Aether saw it all, before the couple did. He suggested that Oldryn take Zahnah for a long journey, to learn about Heaven. Provisioned for seven orbits or about ten days.

They would ride on the backs of the Clesteny, birds of high intelligence, with a forty- foot wingspan. They looked like eagles. Saddled up, they took wing, guiding the Clesteny telepathically. In a few hours they landed next to a grand waterfall. This was a marriage place and Zahnah knew without asking. At thirteen feet tall, Oldryn towered over Zahnah. With his muscular body, he weighed four-hundred pounds, with curly golden hair and light green eyes.

The Clesteny sensed the need to remove themselves and once unsaddled, they took off hunting. Marriage was between Life Giver and the two lovers. They need only ask permission and then stand before Life Giver, who then makes the marriage. Mighty Oldryn stood trembling in tears. Fierce Zahnah had a penetrating sense of purpose and stood there in stillness. Life Giver then spoke the words. "I stand with you. The blessing, of marriage, is given. The bonded covenant is ours to protect. We shall always, walk together and I will bless the conceptions of your children." The Voice was audible!

They lay upon the soft grass and Zahnah marveled at the way Oldryn made love to her. His tender, gentle touch was filled with a love that transcended passion. They moved with excitement as her first climax was truly that. After all her orgasms but the last one, they climaxed together with deep groaning. They conceived.

The results were monumental. New life of the highest order, the gift was given, in receipt of perfection. They saw it all so clearly. They would then be amorous, until the Clesteny returned. They made good use of their private time together, in passion. They kept busy for two orbits.

"Eons earlier, when we learned how to face our fears with faith, we discovered what it is to be free. The Angels in this Heaven are physical, the Celestial. We have served with the same dedication and responsibility. We hear the One-God's voice audibly. His voice rings out to us, and you also hear it in this way. While He remains concealed from open view, in the material sense.

"We are the Angelic corollary, in material form. A facsimile in the physical dimension. Both are equally sacred, whether spiritual or material. Soon our extended family will be streaming in. To live on this giant Star. Living as one. Two dimensions of Heaven, also living as one. These dimensions were never meant to be merged, but standing together as one, complimenting each other. The same as we do, my precious Zahnah!" She loved her Oldryn more than seemed possible. To her, he was also a miracle.

Soon, streaming in from everywhere, the Abrahamic seedlings arrived. Aeron of the Celestial, called this time, the Arrival. Similar to Abraham's arrival in the promised land. In the first book of the Jewish bible, Abraham received the command to "Go to yourself and find the place that I will show you." By this He meant, to reflect stillness, to hear His guidance. Life Giver would show His child, the way to the tribal peoplehood, of faithful reliance. To the time of his arrival, at the place where the Lord would show His way, to those willing to walk the path of the living. Past, present and future are one in the eyes of Life Giver. By this reality, the last can be first. Revolutions of lives, incarnations toward perfection, the prophetic wheels of living souls, Gilgulim in Hebrew, flowing in timeless eternity.

This new arrival would bring with it a new revelation of life. All who arrived were making the journey of Abraham, their father. To go to themselves in stillness, opening the floodgates yet again. Revolutions, encircling revelations, as to the way of life. Taught by the One, through all His Abrahamic, Covenant Keepers, from the center of the multiverse, named Jerusalem. For His explicit Divine purpose, to bless generously, from the outpourings of His heart. Aether spoke truth to power, in blessing the gathered throng.

"In the ancient Earth measure of it, our present time would be 14,856 AD. Eons earlier, wondering wanderers, experienced the fusion, of material and spiritual reality. They began living this reality the moment they looked up and out, we know the name Life Giver from them. Before the invention of the wheel, they used Prayer Wheels to help them to see in this fusion. Wheels representing the cycles of knowing. How the singularity of cyclical revolutions, showed revelatory recognition, of the greater vision of reality, unseparated, as single unity.

"These wheels could be looked through, by the eye of the soul, to really see. To add visionary focus. They also designated the seasons, relative to the orbits of various worlds, to their light sources. All based in light transmissions. As measured by orbital light intensities. The cycles of light transmission. Determining the cycles of seasons, and the living cycles in their inhabitants, as to the 'yearly' building of Divine Connection. That hidden in nature, would be revealed, their soul directions, through their life cycles. Connections with both the natural world and the Creator of it all.

"Then more was discovered as they learned to transcend dimensions, in order to enter the consciousness of a totality of dimensions. The visitors, of this reality, found the way of merger, with all dimensionalities, and trans-dimensional travel beyond previous spacetime limitations. Which has led us to discover, that spiritually, we have nothing on our primal forbears, in the apprehensions of reality.

"That only by walking with Life Giver can we know reality. Only by His transmissions of light. For all our discoveries, no matter how great, there is truly nothing but Life Giver. That is the how and the why, that the original Abraham, shows us the way of the living. The original plan, to bring us all together, all those that battled destructive forces through history. To give us the Son. To bless us with life, all of us as one.

All the Abrahamic tribes are one nation now.

Ayoshuah, under your righteousness we stand

That the Lord may view us in your light

By your worthiness, may we be seen

That the Lord may answer our prayer

The name of the Son in Aramaic is Ayoshuah.

The deadly riddle of evil, is about our weapon against it. How we bar its entry. The key is love, given, received and returned, between each other and our Maker. He gave us, the two most vital keys, to service. Love God completely and love each other truly.

Chapter Twenty
A New Nation

After a few centuries had passed, a new name was given, to all of the Abrahamic accord. Yes indeed, the three had evolved into a far greater one! The Human accelerant, with dynamic slingshot effect, had brought them into being, with greater strength in every form. They looked like the Celestial, but with a wholeness, of intelligence, that was startling to behold. They were called Brahim. Their light was meant to be shared and so the new wandering wonderers were a bit of a wonder in themselves.

Showing up anywhere, everywhere, they could serve. It was their highest honor to serve. With delight and laughter and song, they brought love. Both audibly yet concurrently telepathic, like the Amvry. The experience was an ecstasy. They danced with everyone, they taught that through joy, everything is delivered. That joy had deepest healing, in its very nature. Celebration in joy, the truest song of life. Life being the praise, that Life Giver sings to his creation. To sing it back, was to celebrate, with Life Giver. This marriage between life and love, being the greatest gift of them all.

History can be a sad subject. Astraea was a five-year old history buff. When she got to 2023 AD, she became much troubled regarding her ancient ancestors on planet Earth, in America. Soon after the tragic displacements of Covid19, right on its heels, came Covid23, the next biological attack. The time had come to deliver the Trojan Horse of genetic engineering. Injectables, to kill and control, with specified, targeted, global genetic genocide. The fix was in.

The orgy of fear came just in time for the central bankers

next move. The new vaccines were ready. Loaded with contact tracer ingredients, the noose began tightening. The rich-y-poo-poos were ready to rule the world with the tightest iron grip in recorded history. In the vaccines, were nanoparticles, designed to deliver information. Also, in these vaccine injections, were biometric microchips and thus the enslavement could now roll ahead. Next would come the dollar crash, obviating the dire need for a cashless system. Those without the chips could not use the system! They would be destitute. They would starve.

Elections governed by misinformation. Through big tech, bank, news media, pharma and voting machines, marching in lock step. The Tech-narky would rule the Luciferic world. The beast system. A demonic shriek that covered humanity. Fear overruled, analyzing logic, and so the carefully orchestrated stampede for 'safety' was unleashed. They gratefully walked down the plank and jumped into the sea of slavery. They had been injected with all the components needed to rule over them. They had not known how the tiny biochips would become chains. After the crash and death of the dollar, they were told that only the cashless currency system could protect them from financial ruination. They ran to sign up just as they ran to get their vaccines.

The now desperate fools only wanted safety and to hell with freedom. Scared people are unworthy of freedom, and do not want freedom. They prefer to be fleeced, while being reassured they could have peace, prosperity and most of all, safety. Nobody told the sheeple how their innocent behavior would be punished, one day, by cutting off the financial taps of income. Now deranged with blind fear, they were less free than the most pitiful slaves that came before them.

What could they do? The news-media harangue was constant with tales of those who tried to resist. How they were cut down or dragged to the gulags on every continent. Astraea was perplexed. How was it that they did not know? Those without fear are free! How could America of all places, become the land of scared rabbits? This was how the mega-bankers and other megalomaniacs, killed America. Her young eyes were filled with desolation, she could see it all.

During the Tribulation, it was only the warring nations, that provided some cover for those sheltering from all the Luciferic shitstorms. The monsters were too busy killing each other, to chase them all down. Small time criminals could do that. Mankind on trial.

Astraea was flummoxed and sad. At five and fully alive, seeing the depth of darkness for the first time. Her father, Zaida, invited some looney friends, from that era, to brighten things up a bit. They described how Life Giver led them through the shadows of death. How living through those times opened them up to accelerated evolution. How deliverance had been no further away than to ask for it. The pall of despair began lifting from her sweet little face.

Ben, "Look at the beginning of the bible. The genesis of creation. I paraphrase here, 'First, God breathing and speaking into being: light. And that first light that life comes from was tov.' Tov, in Hebrew, is much more than just good. This highest level of good surpasses any English word for it. This level of good describes the light that came before the luminary sunlight. That same good, that describes the Creator, Himself. This light that was tov, was the omnipresent, absolute light, ephemeral. It is this interior light that activates creation."

Walter, "The energizing spark of life. Life is the most powerful force. But this light, is what enlivens it. Life-force energy, impossible to separate from the earliest light, because this light sparks the kindling of life. Met together in creation, they are one. A single force."

Jake, "This realization is a most happy one. Because it describes the absolute dynamism in creation. Because Life Giver's love is spoken into creation, through His breath of the light that engenders life!"

Ben, "God said, 'Let there be light' and from that formative light preexisting any other, He created all that is. Our connection with our living Creator, is alive, activating our embrace. Our actions are sustained by His aliveness. The gift of taking action by the Hand and the Name of our Father."

Walter, "So when God was hovering over the deep, He was watching over the dawn of creation, with the first light. He was sparkling, or mirachefet, energizing the waters. Hovering with the spark of life. The light energy found in all life. The interior sustaining light from which all life flows. With His Light, He impregnated the deep, with the first: Life!"

Jake, "Some Hebrew words have no equivalent in English. Mirachefet is a creating, divine, energy. An energetic hovering. Love is life to us. From those 'hovering' sparks, that began to fly, within the deep and then life was born. God's watching, over the dawn of creation, with the first light. The inner, primordial, creating, light.

"So, little one, as they say, 'The metal was ready for the Maker's Hand.' But this creative sword, our Messiah, the Son, is no material sword. It is the staff of our Shepherd, by the desire of the Father. Those tough times that you were studying about, were self-made nightmares. They were killing themselves through their indifference toward their creator. They fed the fear that they were killing themselves with. Had they turned back they would have seen this light we speak of. The darkness would have subsided. If they could have seen your face, they could have regained their innocence. In your face, I see Life Giver."

After those resurrected men left, Astraea said to Zaida, "Those men were silly, while speaking seriously. Perhaps their humor buoyed them from despair. How brave they must have been." The little rascal was onto something there! To live we must have light and water, these grow the bread of our sustenance. Love is like the nurturant earth and the air we breathe. Spirit gives us the inspiration to live well. These five elements are gifts from beyond what we know.

Little five-year old Astraea had a monumental intellect. She could not fathom evil. She did understand how much destruction came from it. In her mind, she understood evil, while in her heart and soul, she felt its chilling effects. She was too pure a soul, to fathom it. For over eleven-thousand years, no one had seen it. Had she been born under the yolk of its enslavement, she would have opposed it, but not fathom it.

Only by being constantly under attack and fighting demons, could she fathom the absolute and malignant stench of it. It is an absolute force! Only by getting some of it on her, in battle, could she fathom it. How the cross of Jesus, was like a sword, to deliver the innocent from evil. She would have been as innocent as she is 'today.' Now all that lives, has evolved beyond having a vessel for it. The past was bloody awful. Evil would never again have a place to live. We have immunity to it. This pathogenic terror exists only in the bitter past. We are living in deep connection. That was the ingredient that rendered us immune, while in the cosmic war. Many died but only for three 'days,' or less. We are risen from death. Little wondrous Astraea skipped along her path. A beauty to behold.

Long ago Jake said, "The deadly riddle of evil, is about our weapon against it. How we bar its entry. The key is love, given, received and returned, between each other and our Maker. He gave us, the two most vital keys, to service. Love God completely and love each other truly.

"Evil creeps in, when we invite it, by our fearful weakness. It is like bait. It is a parasite feeding on the spiritually weak and sickly. Upon a host that will not fight for good. Fearful passivity opens the floodgates. Families destroyed by those who fail to ask Life Giver for help. For example, 'Help me Father, to protect my family and my country. To keep indifference out of our hearts. To stand up for You, our lives and our freedom.' Father, Son, Sacred Wind and the Kingdom of Heaven, with all the Angels, are waiting for you to ask for help.

"Back in 2020 AD, the people had truly lost their way, by letting their fears rule them. The Bill of Rights and Constitution made it clear that freedom and liberty are the law of God. Another Black Robe Regiment was clearly overdue. To teach the way of life, to any willing to listen. To fight alongside the faithful, with honest might.

"However, the people were indifferent to God, life and freedom. They were too corrupt to hold honest elections. They had no respect toward their institutions. Demon fruit was the result. The people conceded to their utterly false politicians. They believed that their votes would never be counted fairly.

"Missouri Senator, Hollings, got it right when he said, regarding the manipulated vote tabulators, designed to receive electronic hack attacks, 'The devil has been playing his fiddle here and if you cannot see it, then you are already asleep in death. Absolute treason has infected all of America. Some kind of revolution of consciousness is required if we are ever to win back our freedom! '

"The nation was in revolt. They wanted their freedom back. It started with regional turmoil between blue and red states. Secessions of states were allowed without challenge in order to avoid the open conflict of war. Again, fear was in charge. Blue states wanted more structure in their governmental model, in order to provided social justice and preserve the people's wellbeing. To be more caring and provide the means to do that. To be kinder toward other nations as well.

"The blue states wanted to secede from the 'union.' Texas was the first state to draw up the articles of secession. They led the other red states that wanted a genuine return to the founding principles. A revival of the American way of life. Sadly, it was all a circular firing squad. Then our weakness did draw an attack. China could not resist. Although America would very nearly die, she would yet be reborn from the ashes.

"Small but deep rivers. Small but deep creeks. The spring fed cleansing waters of life, would yet return. With it, reliance on our Maker. From the bowels of despair, freedom would rise again. When we returned to our Father, He fought for us. After the blue states collapsed, they ran back into the union. God makes blind, those who walk to destruction. The blue states suffered terrors and losses far greater than the red states.

"Just as Pharaoh refused to let God's people go, the USA refused to let God's people go. Hence the great collapse. Until they blinked. Freedoms resurgence brought them back to the Promised Land. We became America again. As a unified country, we learned once again, to love our Maker and to truly love each other. Later on, the world lost about eight billion people, in the curse, of the real walking dead, also known as the Great Tribulation. Where we were learning again, Who, was the boss of the universe, and to love Him and to truly love each other. God always wins. At the end of the Great Tribulation came the Great Blessing!"

Flying is at the core of our ways. First of all, never 'try' to do anything. Just let it happen. By looking where. See clearly the where, with the eyes of your soul. That's it, that's our way. Keep going as long as you like, and bring me along with you, past space-time and through the Wraith.

Wraith of Realms flight is trans-dimensional travel. It comes from a willingness to merge multi-dimensionally, with respect to what discovery your soul wishes to encounter. We had disappeared from sight the moment that we leapt. Beyond the mind, lies a multiverse of experiential travel.

Chapter Twenty-One
Closer To Our Maker

Among the next worlds to be discovered, were a great many ultra-luminous ones. Each one bringing us closer to our Maker. Several ships of the Brahim, found themselves rising quickly, into a shimmering silver brightness. Through tendrils of multi-dimensionalities. Somehow, we Brahim, were out of our ships and into the loving embrace of beings who seemed to be most fascinated with their new friends. Welcomed, as revered family members, and intensely gazing into us with unequaled, visionary, depth. Laughing with a celebratory, yet gentle demeanor. We were spellbound by all this and went with it, while filled with wonder.

Their telepathic voices were sincere and kind. For them it seemed that life was a constant reverie of contact and newfound realizations. They inhaled discovery. Their desire was to encounter all reality as a gifting, teachable, moment. Not really physical or perhaps made of both material and spiritual fabric. More like Angels, really. But with enough physical heft to hold and carry their large new friends. Wait a moment! How is that possible? How could they pick up and run with a four hundred-pound Brahim?

Oeskar of the Ruy, said to me, "Aundeiri, of the Brahim, your curiosity, rivals mine. We Ruyin are propelled by the energy of our thought. So, by our desire, comes the energy to make it so. We stand in several dimensionalities, just as do Angels. Technically, we are physical, but we move in and through the celestial, ethereal, Wraith of Realms. Like the ancient Chiricahua, moving into the transmissive portal of their medicine wheels and through their new eyes, as given in vision quest. They had to really work at it, while for us it is second nature. We can bounce between dimensions as quickly as our souls look 'there.' We look like Angels, but we can shape shift at will. Skin-shifting into invisibility. That's how we have been visiting you during the eons of your development. Knowing how Life Giver favors you, really piqued our interest. We find your single species, throughout time, most comical. We also love you!"

I said, "We all felt your love instantly. That you have been loving us clear back to our primal, cave dweller, beginnings. We keep running into older and older species as we rove further and further throughout space. Does this anomaly coincide with a greater law? The further we go out there, the older, are the civilizations?" Oeskar was really cracking up! He was roaring with audible laughter.

"Gee, do you think so? I'm sorry but how did you miss this?" He began play, wrestling with me, in comradery. We'd known them only for minutes and yet we were brothers. "You Angel looking dudes are ornery. You have known us intimately, yet only now are we beginning to know ourselves."

"That is because we've been around for trillions of years. Here, let me show you what we looked like in our early forms." They looked like fish, living in streams. Then they looked like amphibians, then reptiles, then birds. Then bird-like mammals that stood upright and so on until they reached their current ephemeral state.

"I really like your wings, but now you just float around, when do you fly around?" "When we feel like it, just like everything else!" Then, with me in his arms, he leapt into graceful flight. But we were also flying through dimensionalities, that he called the Wraith of Realms. All these dimensions were connectedly merging, as in this travel, they all seem to be one. Or at least I experienced them as one. Oeskar seemed to think that I was childlike in my wonder. Then he said, "Hanging out with you, I can clearly see why Life Giver has favored you, throughout your history. He told me that you have been formed, literally, out of Himself. In terms of both spiritual and material DNA."

"Sons and Daughters," I said. Then he, "Yes, you believe that now, but look how you were as a species, always running away from that knowing, and the responsibility, that it entails." "We developed, under sin, so slowly, that when we were finally ready to face the music, all hell broke loose. The bad stuff had built up a lot of pressure."

"That is because actions generate huge amounts of spiritual energy, both positive and negative."

"Historically, it's no wonder you found us so amusing, as we blundered about, trying to find our way. All the while refusing the guidance available to us."

"But you've been wasting no time for the last twelve thousand Earth years. You are ready now, for that which is to come. You can see, that our celestial, ethereal conveyance, is moving by our will. Sending us through the transmissive Wraith of Realms. Moving us wherever we look. Elemental on the spiritual planes. Our soul-seeing vehicles take us to constant discovery. We welcome you to stay with us as long as any of you wish. As royalty, by your Divine inheritance, we commit to you, anything you may wish."

"When the student is ready, the teacher will appear. I, Aundeiri, of the Brahim, stand with the Ruyin, for as long as it takes to learn your ways. Firstly, your ways of flying."

"Of course, you have chosen well, as flying is at the core of our ways. First of all, never 'try' to do anything, just let it happen, by looking where. Seeing clearly the where, with the eyes of your soul...that's it, that's our way, keep going for as long as you like, and bring me along with you, past spacetime and through the Wraith."

Then we went together for a very long time. At the start, I envisioned glorious wings of great span, to leap as Oeskar had. He yelled telepathically, "You are amazing, this stuff comes easy for you, more easily than it did for me. Once you experience, you see the how, and off you go!"

The Wraith of Realms is just a willingness to merge multi-dimensionally, with respect as to what discovery your soul wishes to encounter. I sang audibly, with my deepest voice, this was true paradise for me and Oeskar wept tears of joy. This was mine. As 'pilot,' in command, nothing was in my way, as the distance grew greater. We had disappeared from sight, to any that we knew. Words, of any language, cannot describe the magnitude, the spectacular... I was also, gently weeping, with a still, ecstatic peace. Beyond the mind, lies a multiverse of experiential travel, for those who can keep the doors open and free of thought or analyses.

We had been gone for so great a 'time,' that everyone ran to see us. "We went beyond questing, we just went, and now, we are starving!" After feasting and sharing copious amounts of Nomiruan wine, we slept the sleep of the just. Ruyin flying, yielded intense satisfaction. Its physical corollary might be described as having wonderful lovemaking with your wife and conceiving a blessed child. When Oeskar heard my thoughts, as everyone did, including my wife and children, we laughed uproariously. I had learned that the dance of life included the most wonderful flying. I chose, to keep my wings, which meant sleeping on my belly. My bride, Lurynda, said that my wings were irresistibly sexy!

"Tell me of your beginnings, your history, Aundeiri of the Brahim?" I answered Oeskar.

"I have been the Teller, the Keeper of histories, of the Brahim and our ancestors. To provide an elemental overview, across the span of the most recent twenty thousand years, in three small books. A glimpse into the general tale. To tie together what occurred. I was born a Hunomiruan Being, long before our evolvement into the Brahim. Active in battle, I was conceived on an Alliance ship. A Singer for almost the entire battle, of the Thousand years. A warrior opposing evil. After the Thousand, I began traveling back to the origins of the Human, Nomiruan, Celestial, and Brahim.

"It was all so amazing! How early Earthers, Nomiruan, and

the Celestial, all had virtually the same beginnings. How Life Giver always intended to make us one. Tracing my own ancestry, of Jake, Walter, Eleazar, Sam, Naomi, Flux, and Zahnah, to their origins, as a paradigm reference, for entry into the study of all beings of the Abrahamic Covenant Keepers. Therefore, the first book started with the story of Earth. The second, about the interplay, among the species. The third is only half written. I will speak of you, my newest best friend and teacher, and all that is to come. Until our Maker tells me, that it is done.

"Lurynda and I and our children, are a fusion of the Abrahamic peoples. While I am over twelve thousand years old, Lurynda, of the Brahim, is but twenty-eight. She and our children are life itself to me.

"Our newly learned, way of flying, can couple all dimensions together, to allow for unimaginable discovery. I will give all the new pilots, an old and venerated name: Singers!"

Oeskar, deeply moved, said this, "It is an honor to take on the teaching, of all your new Singers. However, you have already surpassed me, in just your first flight. It seems that you may have been called to teach the most advanced, and probably quite soon. Life Giver truly calls for you. To become a most powerful, dimensional traveler. Augmenting your story telling, in so many unforeseen ways."

Indeed, the vast, inter-dimensional distances, were becoming intimately close! Soon, new realizations, would seep into the consciousness of all those in deep connection, inside the Web of Being. Aundeiri's children would be more powerful than he. As was Lurynda. Also, she was taller than he. Their children would tower over him, in more ways, than one! They would form the New Guild of Singers. In time, all Brahim, would join. Pilots in no need of ships. The endless expanse was becoming a cozy little neighborhood. The inner technologies prevailing.

Aundeiri spoke with Lurynda and their children, during their Shabbat. He began telling them about his conversations with the resurrected Jake, and how he began to quote his Creator long ago, when he was physical, "Sadly, America chose the path of the fallen. Triggering their collapse and with it came the Great Tribulation. Starting in a curse, while ending, in the Great Blessing. You took action, helping others, through that time."

He spoke of the story of Ben Hur. Written by a Confederate General, Lew Wallace, who later became the Governor of New Mexico Territory and how it got him to thinking...

"While in one of my reveries, I was struck by the similarity of ancient Egypt, ancient and more recent Rome, the Germany of Hitler and then more recently, the revived Holy Roman Empire of Europe, co-led by the Vatican and the Antichrist strongman, of Germany. All brought holocausts upon the Jewish people.

"Even their salute, with arm extended slightly up, as performed by the ancient Romans, the Germany of Hitler, and the fascist dictatorship of Mussolini. All their salutes were the same. It also became the salute of the end time global government, just as it had been, the salute of ancient Egypt! These megalomaniacal salutes were universal.

"Ancient Egypt and then Rome, lived in fierce hatred of the Jews. Then the German Reich, with the Vatican in cahoots. Then Germany's Antichrist and the Vatican Pope, once again sought to oversee the final solution of the Jewish problem, since the killing of Jews by many nations, left some, as not yet exterminated. Demographically, without the killings, there would have been at least three-hundred- million Jews, alive at that time.

"By the way, Jake is one our ancestors."

Then Jake continued quoting his Maker, "Your entire life has been a miracle. You met, as a child, the Man from Heaven, My Son. Who became manifest in Human form, to be the sinless covering of sin, and thus provide shelter for those who seek to return, or enter, into a living relationship, with Me. To open a conduit between Me and all of My children.

"When you were little, you were in terrible need of comforting. You were a sensitive lad. You found My Son, as He was following after you. To help you see Him. You have been in My keeping ever since."

Then Jake went on speaking about spiritual body language, "Lifting a hand outward, palm down, as a display of power, has a chilling charge to it. Emitting from themselves, as the power source, in order to play God, with Satanic assistance. They are channeling the darkness. Palms up, is a willingness to receive from God. Hands lifted high, speak of connection and allegiance with our Maker. Unless we lower our hands with palms turned back toward ourselves, trying to grab some of that power, and leading toward a delusional sorcery, found in many a large church.

"Long ago, the world was divided, against God. Because the actual power of God would annul their false power, limiting their authority. Men worship God or else they worship power. Although God made man in His own image and likeness, soon he went astray, further and further, from his own essence. The Lord puts the future in our hands, either to bless it or curse it. Shall we not rise to meet the day? Or do we hide in our night to prey on others? It was early on that man began to play God."

Aundeiri shared all of this vintage Jake with his family, because the afternoon of Shabbat, is the time to spend pondering, in the ways of Life Giver.

Over the next few centuries all Brahim were trans-dimensionally flying. It was a matter of duty to do so. Closely on the heels of that, came the general use of this level of consciousness. All living beings burst forth into the fusing of realms. Moving ever closer to perfection. Connection with Life Giver and with all life forms, in all their dimensions, as a part of taking responsibility, for the deepening of reality. Yielding a greater intimacy with 'others,' across the community of the living.

Reality is fluid quicksilver. Flowing in constant change. Permeable, one into every other. The very nature of reality is multifaceted. Its very nature, a balancing of influence. A variability, looking through a kaleidoscope, into the prisms of alternate realities. Lenses of realms, each altering, to every other past-present-future.

In timeless change. Trans-dimensional influence of physical reality.

Changing, transforming,transcending, according to the way realities are experienced. Reality is elastic. As are dimensions, space-time-matter continuums, spiritual realms, and the way we experience them. Various beings will experience their own, unique, reality.

When the material is in balance with the spiritual, it is thus possible, to grow literal wings, by the force of our spiritual wings. A new reality can then evolve wings, with a new genetic structure, to provide for them.

Chapter Twenty-Two
Back To The Beginning

Going forever into the past and future lends a resonance to our lives. A more resonating experience with awareness. The cumulative, shared experience across spacetime-dimension. Ruyin and Amvryin among many others, boarded Brahimian ships, to continue our search. It is in our nature to go exploring. All Brahim love to do this. Our ancestry is filled with this restless, creative force within. The Wandering Jew, whose chosen inclination, calls for constant action. Life Giver stamped Abraham, with both a longing for encounter in hearing Him, and the compelling need to take action, upon His guidance. Exploring is in our genetic code. When asked, "Where are you", our response is, "Right here." This internal energy, seemed to get us into and out of, all kinds of trouble. Wrestling with the ways of God. In order to better understand our job, which is to serve! Brahim, are driven by this same creative impulse. To discover! Our next visitation was instantly immediate.

Before we were even near to them, they appeared, within our ship. They stood next to us, throughout the ship. The music of the Amvry was scintillating. As was the music of the Ruyin. Just as was the music of the Fendalyn. They began dancing with 'everybody' on board. Tearful and rapturous, their joy in meeting us. Their concept of the sacred included all of us and this was obvious to us all. These colorful beings were delightful. One of them began to speak.

"We must all go to flight in the Wraith mode, as with your ships, there is too much turbulence, in the dimensional shifting, to be with us on the ground of Timor. Your ships can stay where they are while we visit as many orbits as you may wish. Your ships cannot fly in the Wraith of Realms. Maybe someday, until then you can come and go, by Wraith-flight. My name is Aquellas. Which means in our tongue, Joy. Our name is Fendalyn, which means constant, always there. Like the Hebrew name, Eitan. The name Fendalyn is both singular and plural, as there is no distance between us, in Sacred Unity with Life Giver and between ourselves."

Even in the new way of flying, the distances were vast, inter-dimensionally. These beings had been around a long 'time.' So long, that it was a stretch to picture it. So how old is that? Hard to say. When you get into trillions of trillions!

The Fendalyn had variable solidity. Like the resurrected. You could put your hand right through them, when in their most luminously bright form. Or make themselves as solid and sturdy as the Brahim. Their colors would swirl as an additional aspect of communication. As was their telepathic music. More pronounced when in their most open, ethereal form. Their most prayerful and expansive state. Neon blues, yellows, turquoises, greens, reds, oranges, and purples, with never before seen, new to us, colors. All in flowing hot neon pearlescent luminosity. Without ego, their desire to reveal themselves in conversation, had no qualms of any embarrassment whatsoever. A spiritual and emotional bravery, witnessing Divine Presence in each other, and with no other being excepted. Loving each other and all their new friends.

Though they were transmissive, deep dreamers, they could be truly constant, with color receding in abeyance to their profoundly constant nature. That is where they get the name Fendalyn. By their intensity of purpose, they truly were most resolute indeed. With colors withdrawing, and their outward halos becoming far brighter. They were spiritual warriors. With a still and quiet variant, of the burning magnesium surround. Here, their outward brilliance of the eternal light, was near blinding. That was how strong their will could be when needed. Tough beings can be kind. Strength can allow vulnerability. The most resolute can be the most loving. In short, warriors are kind and tender hearted, lovers of peace.

Their facial features seem to resonate with their character. Large almond shaped eyes of dazzling oranges in the pupils, with irises that are brightly turquoise. Easy to get lost in their gaze.

More about their eyes. Their huge Irises were surrounded by a thin bright blue turquoise line and then a thinner viridian line. The, inner and still huge Iris, was a glistening mix of tiny copper and flamelike sparkle, in the midst of an overpowering splash of oranges, seemingly on fire somehow, with the interminglement of bright burning silvers, coppers and golds. All with undertones of a burning magnesium brightness.

Their pupils were also deep silver turquoise with coppery flames, along with a stronger undertone of that miracle burning magnesium.

Their bodies are almost humanoid. Powerful, muscular and agile, while androgynous. Neither male nor female, they join in coitus, and then both deliver a child. Their offspring are born quite small and are kept in a pouch with tiny breasts inside to feed the young. Inwardly fierce while outwardly serene. During the thousand years war, they had been wildly successful, utterly destroying any foe to come anywhere near them. In their sector of space, kinetic contacts were few and far between. They had fought without any Alliance participation, as they were hidden and secret, in the vast, far flung enormity, where they dwelled. Nevertheless, they ventured deeply enough into the fray, to exact enormous casualties.

Aundeiri spoke with Spark, of the Fendalyn, "God gave life and freedom to all His expansive creation. In grievous misfortune, some chose contraction, the not God force. To control other living beings, enforce their will over them and feed on them in slavery. The spiritual name, of this contraction and its destructive, spiritual energy, is Ha Satan. The adversarial spirit, running counter to life. This, powerful spirit, is the un-creator, the destroyer. That kills with an ultimate venom. The antidote, to the venom, is Life Giver's Son and He is the Hand of Creation."

Spark said, "Your words of truth are simple in their power. Even when your species were brutes, their inclination was to hear the greatest truths. You were made that way, and this making, caused us to take note of you. Even before the first day that man looked up in wonder. For when you sought to truly see and hear, we saw and heard, that the kindling fire, Eternal Flame, of deepest discovery, was your innate gift from beyond. That one day, you would find us, proving your readiness to engage with us. What you might have seen, in picking up a precious gem from the earth, is what we saw, when gazing upon you.

"We now move with you, as we join together in tomorrow. We as one, are becoming a creative force, to further exemplify Life Giver's intention. Moving closer toward actual creating, in harmony with our Maker. We have His trust as we have trusted Him."

Spark and I leapt into our new way of flying, bringing my sweet, powerful, Lurynda. Three of us began together, the unfolding of the possible future, as always dependent on what the created, decide to do. Past, present, future, are so elastic, that what we witness is always based on probabilities. With the only constant being change, among unlimited possibilities.

Discovery in all things and all worlds has been our primary focus, since 3049 AD, when we won the peace. In Earth time the year was 15,049 AD. For twelve thousand years, discovery has been our delight. Those of Brahimian lineage. For many, far longer. As we were streaming through the revelatory lights of discovery, it became clear to us, that Lurynda's presence was shaping somewhat, how we were able to see. For it is the vessel that decides what may fill it. Aundeiri would never again fly without his bride, she brought just so much more, to the experience. Just as past, present and future can be experienced as one, she and I were also to experience, as one. Each of us adding into the vessel of seeing. Trans-dimensional flight is elucidated, as is prayer, by those flying together. By the gifting that we receive together.

Brahimian tradition, calls for a Minyan or joining, of ten or more, to focus the power of prayer. Spark, "Yes, we will join with many together now, in our Sacred flight."

A throng of powerful leaders, from a teeming number of the sacral, leapt together, in Sacred flight. We witnessed together, what appeared to be the Son of Light, our Messiah. To even try to make words about this, would only lessen what we saw. To desecrate the holy. Our change, within us, was magnificent. Prayer has always been about cultivating and refining our vessel. Our service to the Divine, has always been His gift to us. Not for Him, but for service clarifying our growing relationship. He has no need for offering. The love we give to Him, inspires the love that He returns. All things begin with His love, as also they end in Him. We go back to the beginning, when we touch the Divine Altar. This love begins existence. This love is the creating light.

The great flight that we had undertaken, left us still, for a very long time. Utter harmony left us with nothing express-able in words. T'HALLEL YAH, Halle-lu-yah, praise God!

Some children were about to get into the weeds, playing catch with observations about the nature of reality. Powerful brains, little bodies.

"Within the possibility, of evolving dimensionality, reside every alternative. Variants of seemingly, 'normative,' reality. History can thus be seen through multiples. In prisms of realms and dimensions. Multidimensionality is like a looking glass, to peruse historic and prophetic variants of what has been, what is or what will be. To alter any of these, is to change them all. Every level of consciousness, of every living being, is influenced by their predominant streams of reality."

"Reality is fluid quicksilver, flowing, in constant change. Permeable, one into every other. The very nature of reality is multifaceted. Its very nature, a balancing of influence. A variability, looking through a kaleidoscope, into the prisms of alternate realities. Lenses of realms, each altering, to every other past-present-future, in timelines of change. Trans-dimensional influence of physical reality. Changing, transforming, transcending, according to the way realities are experienced. Large and little warps tumble together, evincing those realities, that prevail."

"Reality is elastic. As are dimensions, space-time-matter continuums, spiritual realms and the way we experience them. Various beings will experience their own, unique, reality."

"Evolution is a becoming. Adaptation to reality, as we encounter it. To grow through adversity. Survivability under pressure, as we adapt to live with changing realities. When a species evolves spiritually, they change how they see and thus believe. There can be physical adaptations. Evolving our reality creates change."

"When the material is in balance with the spiritual, it is thus possible, to grow literal wings, by the force of our spiritual wings. A new reality can then evolve wings, with a new genetic structure, to provide for them. Our will enables us to be, what we believe. We are what we believe, as we meet circumstances, created by our belief. When we believe that telepathy is desirable, an evolution to encounter this adaptation, is set in motion. The desire and vessel to receive, eventuates evolution. Mates will be chosen, who have these gifts. Our belief in telepathy can engender an evolution in our telepathic abilities."

"Our scientific breakthroughs can begin to alter our consciousness. Over time our beliefs can trigger genetic evolution. Natural selection in our choices, evolve biologic response. Telepathy can help dramatically in hearing the true intentions of those we encounter, giving us time to move away if we so choose. We choose mates that are exemplary, for this function."

"Put another way, evolution is triggered by belief. Which

evolves adaptations, changing reality. The way we see things, changes the flow of evolution." Kids will be kids! They began kicking history around, all over the place. Brahim children remembered their ancestry.

"The great American Pogroms of 2026 AD, were but a glimpse into Jewish history. Of one mass genocide after another. Always looking down the barrel, of the next mass, monstrous, mess."

"Ever since the first Abraham, was the killing of Jews, as they challenge despotism."

"Those without fear remain free even under slavery and imprisonment. By the power of God. That is what tyrants hate. What Satan hates.

"Jews have been emancipated slaves, ever since ancient Egypt. A symbol of freedom that has been hated by every flavor of fascist since."

"With God breaking the chains of their captivity. As a symbol of those whom God raised up from slavery. Jesus showing up when He did, even dissolving the chains of sin, really drove them crazy!"

"All Jews were free always, throughout our history. Because we lived for something greater than the state."

"It is possible that Rome hated us even more than Egypt. The God of the Jews challenged Egypt to obey God and release them."

"But Rome saw that the Jewish God, was the One who directly challenged their right to exert force over anyone. The Jews of that time knew that Messiah would come, as a conquering King, to overthrow Roman might itself!"

"One even greater than Moses."

"That to kill their Messiah, would kill their hope and make them bow their head to Rome. But that only made the Jews fight harder still. Rome could not kill the freedom their God had bestowed upon them as their literal birthright."

"The battle of Massada, in far greater scale than the Alamo, demonstrated the Jewish will to have God rule over them and no man ever!"

"Challenging the ultimate power of all tyrants forever! How dare those Jews live free? Because they have a Liberator who hates slavery!"

They would not wage war against natural habitat, to enslave it for wealth and power. Native sanctuary for all life, would never again be worked to death for profit. Part of nature, in majesty they walked. Looks like the Indians won after all.

They walked alongside their horses, in the unspoken dignity of their way. They gifted with pleasure, to each other, whatever was needed. There was no buying or selling or trading.

Ownership was over. To try to own, is to use force. Enslaving what they own. Here you gave your favorite horse for the pleasure of giving.

The joke was that horses, like land, could be owned at all. So that the person you gave your horse to, doesn't mind if you take off with him for however long. The Wind Drinkers go where they please. When you are without fear, the wild ones respect you, and will come in close, without fear, to visit with you.

Chapter Twenty-Three
Children Of Tomorrow

Across the entire web of consciousness, the move of the majority of living beings, was back to the land. We found that we could do anything just by flowing consciousness to whatever place or task, that called for change. The web of all existence could be called upon to make things happen, while at home.

In this, the back to the land folks, could call in immeasurable forces. Leaving us free to walk in truth without distraction. Back to the landers were engaged in raising the inner powers to emplace blessing wherever needed. Every living soul had their part in it. In tribal settings, we learned skills, trades and capabilities, to have something to give to our communities, to do our part and help others. To supply the needs of our tribal families.

The Brahim were great lovers of the Spanish Kiger Horse. Some of which were nearly a foot taller than they were in the distant past. An ancient extolled, "Riding a horseback, is like expansive prayer, because when we're riding, all we feel is free! Connected to the ground, upon which we stand. We live the grounding, that they connect us to. We live their connection. By being in close connection with them, we remember our close connection with the entire natural world. Which is, other than our Messiah, the most profound spiritual connection. Because it joins the materiel realm with the spiritual realm."

"Wow!" The horses were really running. The kids weren't asking them to run, they just wanted to. They'd been in the barn during the blizzard and were exploding with energy. Even though the snow was still pretty deep in places. Wyoming still gets glacial, from time to time, in the old measure of it, in 17631AD. Cowboys were still around.

This ranch raised the finest Kiger Spanish Horses. You needed to be cowgirled up sometimes. Because riding horses and cowboys could be a handful. Brahim cowboys and Kiger Horses, that is. Still living on the land. One thing had sure changed. The lyrics of country music had gotten their depth back. They really meant something once again. Hank Williams would have smiled.

Some things don't change much. Redtail Hawks still circled in blessing. The wild mountains were still naturally alive once again. Just as in the real west, it had always been horsemanship and not skill with a gun, that was the real measure of a man. Fourteen thousand years ago, some reminisced that future generations would never again see the west as they had once seen it. Then centuries without human habitation had restored it all. Life is a force that will move in its own way. Then for millennia, folks had left it that way. Nobody would ever again wish to impose violence against the natural world.

They would not wage war against natural habitat, to enslave it for wealth and power. Natural replenishment of native sanctuary for all life, would never again be endangered. Anywhere in America, a person could live off the land, respectfully, with restoration fulfilled. Walking with nature, seeking live council, from all its inhabitants. To preserve the natural world with all its healing of the soul.

The main horse barn was built using live trees. The pole barn concept, but using uncut whole trees, keeping all their branches, was the new way. The center timber was the tallest tree. With close by trees all around it. With cut timber tying together from the center timber to all the others. So that the structural trees could continue living and growing. Yes, the trees that strangled each other, by being too close to each other, were cut for roofing and siding, but only those that would naturally die off. When forestation is too dense, the majority of young trees die in their natural cycle. Respect for the living trees did not work against mindful building.

This barn was huge. A spring uphill from it supplied water. For the structural trees, horses and the Brahim, that lived high up within the barn. Surrounding trees mitigated the fierceness of the winds. The entire structure was held together by hardwood dowels. Designed to flex with the winds and be easily fixed when the growth of the trees produced uneven stresses. Horses were used in the logging and building as well as in the raising of meadow hay, kept in the lower center of the barn, to be fed off during winter.

At night, all the horses would come back into the barn or near it when they sensed predators were near. The Kiger are so intelligent, so keen of ear and nose, that they are hard to tackle as game. They fight as well or better than mules. They have well coordinated tactics. Some mornings, dead cougars or wolves would be found laying about where the horses had killed them. The Kiger are splendid survivors. They scream for help from their Brahimians, when they need it. The mares know when that is. The mares turn inward, in a circle, ready to kick outward. The stallions turn outward, ready to strike and bite. But a pack of wolves or a grizzly bear required Brahimian attention.

They used long spears, notched, to be flung by a throwing sling, the ancient name for these was Atlatl. And a fourteen-foot Brahim, could send a twelve-foot spear, clean through a one-thousand-pound Grizzly. The Kiger were larger than they used to be, at seventeen hands. And yet their amazingly smooth going and agility remained. At seventeen-hundred-pounds, they could take a three-hundred-fifty-pound Brahim to wherever he wanted to go.

The durability and endurance of both horse and rider were legend. They did not like to use saddles, and only used them for work. To hunt, they went out near naked, if it wasn't too cold. They brought a surcingle to haul a moose or whatever they gleaned from their travels. The all leather surcingle was used to attach to a travois to haul the game along, while they walked alongside their horses, in the unspoken dignity of their way. The Native American way. To live fulfilled, as part of nature. In this majesty they walked. Looks like the Indians won after all!

Rae was Cheyenne Indian, Blue Arrow, in their tongue. Very tall and resolute, trained in the medicine ways of her people. Her husband was of Brahimian ancestry. They were both quite slender and stood nearly fifteen feet tall. She taught history in a town not far from Yellowstone Park. One day in history class, Rae Dawn said, "Decades before those Tribulation times, America was dying fast. The rising tide of strangulation, by the iron grip of authoritarian rule, is what very nearly killed America outright.

"From Beijing to Moscow to Brussels, freedom was already a long time dead. The political right in America, would need to show the people how they might get their freedom and thus country back, convincingly, to ever win an election again.

"All the left needed to do was convince the worlds power brokers that they would remain useful puppets. Then together, they would create the certainty that freedom would soon be asphyxiated once and for all.

"Only planetary war saved the remnant of true Americans, sheltering in their mountain fastness." Rae taught history from the heart. Her ancestors were a part of that struggle, ever since the Europeans arrived, in their quest to own everything, her people had been hunted down. All Americans tasted that same bitterness as freedom was being hunted down and rubbed out. Now the Native and Brahim lived together in harmony. Ancient Jews, Blacks and Indians, had all shared the experience of genocidal slavery, the primary symptom of evil.

The story of Rae and her husband is worth telling. They had come to live on the sprawling Kiger Ranch. She taught history, did healings and was also a power throwing instructor. Sending spears, axes, and knives hard, accurate and fast. She also taught archery.

Her husband, Maragan, was master blacksmith and leather

smith. He forged fierce steel for powerful blades. A maker of devastating bows, arrowheads and arrows. He was good with wood also. Menacing and hungry, axes, spears, knives, and piercing Atlatls. His saddles were works of art.

They had met shortly before the Yellowstone caldera blew. When every last animal came flying out of there, headed for Tucumcari, they knew it was time to book on out of there. But then, instead of a planet killer volcano, it just blew magnitude seven, however, it blew like that for over three months!

Rae and her husband rode all the way to the Kiger Ranch. Stopping only to rest the horses, eat, sleep and recover. Their Kigers took them over two hundred mountainous miles in only eight days, and they arrived fresh and ready to do it again. Except for Rae. Her belly was full of baby.

They built themselves a modest wickiup not far from the main barn. She was pregnant with their first child and needed her own private nest. Small enough that Maragan was always near his wife, just where he wanted to be.

Incredibly tough, the both of them, while loving as deep as forever. Gentle souls, living their truth. The other native people on the ranch were Blackfoot, wonderful a horseback since their beginnings. And they celebrated their new arrivals.

Historically speaking, the genocide of the native peoples was like the genocide of the natural world, the wilderness, the wild and perfect sanctuary. They came to force nature to their will as they had the Black slaves. To work it to death for profit. All owners of any kind of slave, come to hate freedom most of all.

In stark contrast to that, everybody living on Kiger Ranch, found their wealth in experience. They gifted with pleasure, to each other, whatever was needed. There was no buying or selling or trading at all. The tribe was family, including the horses.

The accumulating and keeping of any material wealth, was just as sick and dark as trying to own land. Land belongs to itself. Material stuff was made to give, with plenty apprentices to learn how to make more. Ownership was over. To try to own, is to use force, the beginning stages of slavery, ownership enslaves the owned and the owner.

Here you gave your favorite horse for the pleasure of giving. The joke was that horses, like land, could be owned at all. Like trying to own an eagle or an elk. Ownership is a sickness. So, the person you gave your horse to, doesn't mind if you take off with him for however long.

To prize a great horse, or anything else, is the glory of strong appreciation. Trying to own it, derives no real pleasure, because it is a trap, for our hearts and souls. Just go riding and bond once and forever in friendship. That's the whole package. Our ancestors once were riders of the Spanish Horse, the Kiger. As we are today.

The truest prize is to love, and then sharing is a wonder. Anyway, thousands upon thousands of Kigers are thundering about wherever they feel like. The Wind Drinkers go where they please. They belong to the places where they live, that keep changing with wherever the best grass is to be found. Except for the older and more fragile, along with mares ready to foal and all their colts and fillies, when they are small. They like to stay close to where people are, to be protected and fed and sheltered by them. The fast horses are hard to catch, when other critters are trying to eat them.

Foaling mares and their foals all seem to like staying close to their Brahimians, who care for them because they love them. The horses are family too.

When a predator has a full belly, he may still crave contact with a Brahim, who, by staying put, invites the critter in for a visit. This was one of the most favorite of pass times. Wolves and cougars can be quite sociable. When you are without fear, they respect you, and will come close, also without fear. Sometimes an old wolf becomes a companion to a Brahim. They get lonely.

Kicked out of their wolf family, they join the Brahim. Young wolves also, at times. When they are lost or just too inquisitive not to come close. Watch out for the mommas, whether cougar, wolf or bear.

Evolution was created, to cycle the continuance of creation. It is impossible to contain reality within fixed boundaries.

We turn around back to life after we die. Cycling the flow, in the Presence that sustains life continually.

Spirit joins matter, to be whole. We cannot know or begin to hold it all, unless we die, long enough, to go into the life stream, showing what is total reality.

We reemerge reborn, having taken the cleansing, of living waters. In deepest slumber, she entered his dream state, in penetrative simplicity, with vital soul guidance.

What is ethereal, celestial, ephemeral. By moving through the wraith of these, we lift the veil. Finding ourselves free of limitations.

The gift of freedom continues to manifest in ever greater freedom. He is holding the light of guidance, as we walk together.

Chapter Twenty-Four
Every World Is Eden

Auhousti said, "We need only to return to ourselves to find Eden, each awakening day. By always going back to the beginning, to sanctify it, making ourselves worthy to breathe in life. Worthy to open every door. To bless the path to our source and love our neighbor. Prayer can be simple, like, 'Thank-You Father, I do feel protected by You." Her infant son looked into her eyes with the euphoria that children have. He loved to feel what she was speaking.

"The Priestly function, calling out to God for the people, is contrasted by the Prophets function, calling out to the people, giving the messages from God, as the two sides cycle in the whole of life." He was wiggling and breathily singing so softly.

"Evolution was created, to cycle the continuance of creation. We see adaptive change wherever we look. It is impossible to contain reality within fixed boundaries. The creation that we are, each of us, is always changing as we broaden our vision, and with it, our reality." He was rapturously bouncing around. Feeling the excitement that she was generating.

"Extinctions are followed by the next generations, on the evolutionary trail. Exchanging new life that replaces lesser forms. Evolution is proof of God, as is creation." Could he hear the truth of it?

"We turn around back to life after we die. Because our souls do not die but return again back to the Source. From life to greater life, as the soul evolves. Cycling the flow, in the Presence that sustains life continually." He was quieter now. Hushed.

"The dimly lit notion of any separation, obscures the reality that spiritual energy lights the room, is Divine in nature, in us and all around us." He was sleeping softly.

"People in love, stand in the place where their lifeforce energies merge. Where spirit joins matter, to be whole." He was still listening to her.

"Beauty, reality, are in the eyes of the beholder, as they are united through experience. The God's eye view is inclusive of it all. We cannot know or begin to hold it all, unless we die, long enough, to go into the life stream, showing what is total reality. We reemerge reborn, having taken the cleansing, of living waters."

Although deeply sleeping, he was still taking it all in. Diving into water, he would always feel reborn, that was the point. To feel that way in his every step, to see and hear as one reborn again. While in his deepest slumber, she entered his dream state, with vital soul guidance.

Wonder upon wonder: the true nature of reality. This home world had beings as gentle and loving as the Eritraean.

A quiet place, almost still. Yet the movement here, internally, was at a high order of magnitude. They were gracefully noble yet meek and humble. Not physically powerful but inwardly so. Small and thin with large craniums, and eyes to match, and having a very strong presence. Their dull grey skin was almost demure without anything that would catch the eye. Small and reflective, with such a fierce level of deep sincerity, that it almost hurt. Yes, they were compelling, to say the least.

We visitors were astonished by the penetrative simplicity and depth of them. Free and without any fear, they felt no need to protect themselves at all, in any way. They existed to fulfill their purpose of seeing, hearing and feeling, singular, in that alone. Going anywhere with all that singularity contained. Their very quiet, hushed others, even children. Bringing others into that single, meditative inclination.

A shimmering effect from ground level to three feet, mirage like, as though the energy was in flux there, made movements that could easily be seen, without any color for the contrasting energy waves. As though temperatures were undulating, but it was something else... this small world, no bigger than Earth, was austere in a way similar to these beings.

As soon as we disembarked, the Amvryin leaped off every shoulder, running and squealing with excitement. They were on these new beings as fast as they could get there. The dull seal grey of the Sauhter, People, in English, began to burst out in kaleidoscopic yellows. As did their eyes. The Sauhter were holding the Amvryin in their arms like little babies that were emitting sounds of utmost pleasure. And the Sauhter were singing back to them. Unusually synchronous, they fastened on to one another. On the inside they were much alike, feeling joy in being with each other.

The Sauhter were beings of reverberating depth. The content of that depth is filled with a clear grasp of the actual nature of life. Feeling the flow of its wonder, exhilarating, spontaneous inspiration. The breath of life is made of this. But they, like every other, had lived through a time of great darkness.

Auhousti of the Sauhter spoke to Aundeiri of the Brahim, "As the saying goes," 'Evil is the foul excrement of the well digested souls of the innocent, after being caught in the web of lies.' But it is so much more. It is also the spirit of death.

"Our ancestors wrote about the Death Walkers, for example, 'Never let them make you angry.' Just see who they are without letting them see who you are. They deceive insidiously, it is information warfare. Receive their information cautiously, while intimating that you don't really have any intelligence information of your own. But move softly here. You may be able to misinform them, thankfully, most demons are dumb. However, do not underestimate the lethality of their dark energy, it powers death."

Aundeiri, "Still, the meditative quality of your race put you in good stead, to weather the storm. My race tended to just jump in recklessly at the worst of times. Never adequately testing the waters before jumping in. As a result, we died with our swords in our hands."

"You were a warrior species, just look at You now. We are four feet tall and timid. You are fifteen feet tall and brave. We operate in differing varieties of courage, toward the same goals. We just have different ways of fighting. Your King David exemplifies our way. Using a shepherd's sling to slay a giant. We both rely on Life Giver. And we both love each other."

He picked her up in his arms, holding her as if she were his mother or daughter. A sweet intensity. The Brahimian ships left these kind and deliberate beings wistfully, as they had been to them, the breath of stillness and wholeness. Their hosts had also enjoyed the visit. Finding their guests to be exciting.

Aundeiri and Lurynda were engaged in some pillow talk. "I've been scribbling down a sort of elemental telling of history. Three little books of the general tale, to tie together in overview, what happened. As a Teller and Keeper of history."

She laughed with delightful light heartedness, and said, "So our Brahimian ancestry can be at the core of telling, for all species? How we all begin as pitiable waifs, just struggling to stay alive. How we all eventually find ourselves standing in magnificence."

She was much too smart for him at times. She intuited all of it with ease, while he really had to work at it. "How we are all heading to a rendezvous with Heaven. One step at a time. For that is the true nature of history. The evolution of the species, all of them."

She laughed again, "So what is ethereal, celestial, ephemeral. By moving through the wraith of these, we lift the veil. Finding ourselves free of limitations."

"God's gift of freedom continues to manifest in ever greater freedom. He is holding the light of guidance, as we walk together."

She liked visiting with her lover boy. He was a bit slow, but always there at the finish line. "Outer Space is gradually becoming fully illuminated, like everything else, in God's evolutionary stream of creation, the natural law of life! Like a mirror of all soul's evolvement! To eventually be completely illuminated with the interior light of creation. Shining brightly out past tomorrow."

"Although I don't know how or when, the three little books will be finished, it feels like they may never be. The ending will be called by the voice of Life Giver, or not at all."

Their next stop was going to be a doozy!

Flying Wreath of Realms, required absolute trust. The act of letting go, in trust, is the dynamism required to get the whole picture. Another form of travel was ancestral travel.

Our abilities are on loan. Not ours, they are flowing through us. Beings were coming into view, made of pure light. What language do we use to communicate with pure light?

Turns out, no language. Pure light just is. The conversation is to experience it, and to be experience by it.

Just to stand with them. Be with them. As our eyes and souls began to adjust to them, we began to feel their affection for us.

Could it be that the greatest distances of all, were internal? The soul is our inner eye!

Chapter Twenty-Five
Follow The Light

Those vast reaches of darkness, where the light of suns, are rarely found, somehow lost the blinding effect of pitch black. No, not through thermal, shipboard devices, like before. In the vast, cold, dark, thermals were useless anyway. Except in seeing dark planets, to avoid slow velocity collision. At higher velocities, collision avoidance was handled by folding space. The phenomena that sends space and obstacles around the speeding airfoil.

God's face, to light the way, increased exponentially, as He drew near, as He had always done for those that relied upon Him. For those with the vessel to receive, He drew water from His well. In short, space was getting brighter.

Solary of the Brahim, "Could the presence of Heaven be drawing closer to us all? It seems as though everywhere is returning back to Him." His wife retorted, "Gee, honey, do you think so?" Teasing was common as we merged with the great, unending, beyond. 'Passing the time,' was an inadequate phrase. Perhaps passing the timeless, is closer to it. Endless quiet, expanding outward, still held us somewhat in awe.

However, we were not following the light. It was everywhere. The humbling realization here, is that the light is really following us, and that, as the result of our seeking it! And that, as the result of Life Giver seeking us. For a merger, that while keeping all creation distinct, it would nevertheless, keep dynamic intimacy. That most ancient of phrases, 'There is nothing but God,' might be put, 'There is nothing without God.'

Then suddenly, gradually, it began getting so bright that we were almost blinded by it. Solary said meditatively yet urgently,

"All consciousness aboard ship, let go and move with this, or we may not make it through these shifting dimensionalities. The danger is being left behind, for those hanging on too tightly. Focus on Life Giver." He had not mentioned the scary part about being left behind. How you could cease to exist. Left behind in nothingness.

A soul departure to nowhere left only erasure! Where the evil all went to, long ago. Fortunately, no one, was left behind. But these were as yet unknown dimensionalities. Flying Wreath of Realms, these were still radically new places. Requiring absolute trust, in order to see them. The act of letting go, in trust, is the dynamism required to get the whole picture. Finding actual reality is the grandest prize!

Beings were coming into view, but they were made of light...pure light! What language do you use, to communicate with pure light? Turns out, no language. Pure light just is. The 'conversation' is to experience it and to be experienced by it. Photographic but not physical. A camera could make the picture of it. This experience charged our batteries, our energy envelopes, in ways we were yet to discover. But to speak about the wordless is nearly impossible.

The real message was just to stand with them, be, with them. As our eyes and souls began to adjust to them, we began to feel their affection for us. We had crossed another border together, on our evolutionary trail. As we waved good-bye, their love was sending us on our way. Could it be that the greatest distances of all, were internal?

We could not remember our ships landing anywhere. Our ships logs showed that we had not. We just showed up. Or they arranged for us to meet with them somewhere. But where in the heck? Had we become nonphysical, or partly so? Were they? Or did we go together to meet in our togetherness. We laughed because what ever it was, it was wondrously the best. We did not need to over think it. It just was, and we were glad for it. We laughed ever onward, on the odyssey, to everywhere.

We did crave to stand on the living, breathing ground again. Hyperspace on hyperdrive, returned us quickly. Like Vikings on magic boats, we returned laden with treasure. It was always so good to be home. Wanderlust, fortunately for us, was not constant. Our treasured adventures paled before the treasure of home.

Many of the married couples were with child and nesting was a priority. There is no place like home. We expand more at home and through our dreams, than we do by hauling ass into the even more unknown. The Brahim are a roving species, but we are also a coming home species. Warriors in love with peace.

Another form of travel was ancestral travel. These excursions bore sweetest fruit.   For in the halls of life beyond time, grow the trees of ancestry. Where our ancestors are alive as ever, with open arms. Aundeiri was over fourteen thousand years old, in the prime of his adulthood. Anciently, this time came at forty, the time to study the mysteries, Kabbalah.

Some ancestors are reborn to the Heavens, while some are resurrected, to finish their work. But the ancestral living trees, are the when and where of what has been, what may be. To know them in their own beginnings, was the purpose of returning to them, in their ancestral tree. One can also visit their tree, of the knowledge of good and evil, for perspective. How they fulfilled their purpose, relative to that.

Aundeiri would make the journey to meet them all, to eat the purple flower. Dreaming across the waters of life. To join with them. To see and feel them on every branch of the ever- living tree of life, of his people.

He would also visit the tree of those to come, especially his wife and children, and their progeny. Without time suspension these journeys might last centuries. When he was done, it would feel to him like even more than centuries. All of the full magnitude of all of this, took only the ten hours that he slept.

He would thus see Brahimian, Celestial, Nomiruan and Human history into the past, present and future. It would take him one full moon cycle, to vacate the total thrall of all of this and return to something more similar to his usual state, but he was changed forever!

He had visited the places of life, for all the people's ancestry, of all who were close to him now. After the festival of his return, the Brahim would touch him and say, Amayn, or in English, Amen. And everyone wanted to touch and be touched by the sacrament of his journey.

Here was a bed of riches glowing in the life-stream of living waters. Here on the streams bed of sand and pebbles, lay glowing, vast treasures. Treasures of peoplehood. All his lineage included all the lineage of the ones, who touched him, even distantly, as trees reaching out to other trees and thus to all, in the fullness.

He had peered into every soul, that his soul emanated from, including our Maker. Couples that conceived their children, together with Gods involvement, whether they saw this or not. Every soul before Aundeiri, in every realm of time, had their place in his soul and they were all wondrous to him. Tears beyond joy filled him. He could never forget any part.

Leaping through the veil, into the much beyond consciousness, a transcending phenomena, to places no ship could fly to. Ancestral time travel issued forth from it, how involved Life Giver is. How He was the most vital part, in the make-up of our souls.

His total connection with every soul He crafted. The fulfillment of their lives as part of His own.

Chapter Twenty-Six
How Far?

Such were the journeys of the soul. Some 'day' nothing would be hidden. Ancestral time travel issued forth from it, how involved in every instant, Life Giver actually was, is, ever shall be. How He was the most vital part, in the make-up of our souls. We are a part of Him, as He is a part of us. Seeing that more clearly is central to the evolution of the soul. Life is nourished by truth. Life has a most powerful basis, that of where it comes from. That truth is where we rest in trust. He has never been hidden. Though once we hid from Him. As we evolve, we cease the hiding. For example, His miracles, we must feel them in order to see them! Until we trust, we cannot feel. Until we feel, we cannot see.

Having seen into the deepest regions of those souls in connection with Aundeiri gave him a clearer picture of Life Givers total connection with every soul that He crafted. With the depth of His love for them and commitment to them and the fulfillment of their lives as part of His own. An amazement at this total intimacy with every life as generated from our Makers love for His creation and the signal accomplishment of further perfection on all levels, by the further genesis of their every evolution.

It was here that Aundeiri began to see the children of Lurynda and himself. In the mirroring of all else that he had just seen. The families in creation by the Single Hand. How nations as well are formed through this Divine planning. How Abrahamic families all, had derived from single root. By the name of Abraham. How it did not seem to Aundeiri, at this moment, that he could ever love them more. Yes, he would, just the same. He had gained the understanding that might help him to finish the third little book. How history was beginning to really shine for him.

They now had two daughters and three sons. They all could manifest hugely powerful wings and leap together as family, in wreath of realms flight. Leaping through the veil into the much beyond, consciousness. To places no ship could fly to. All seven of them flying in single consciousness as multiplied by the powers of each to make the whole. At first moments they seemed to themselves quite physical. They really did not know that a transcending phenomena, was taking place, over the place where these "rules" apply. So enthralled in their experience, that conjecture to analyze had no place at all for them. This root of Abraham, to open himself in God's guidance, without doubt or question, was still bearing fruitfulness and multiplying.

They would have many more children together and swarms of grandchildren. With lives exceeding one-hundred-twenty-thousand- of years, time, this was nearly unavoidable. To the rafters of any home, would well be filled with generations of fully adult offspring. Audeiri's army.

Using the enormous transport ships of the past was still practiced, mostly to bring "Noah" cargoes teeming with plant and animal life from various billions of home worlds. Sometimes bringing settlers seeking total emersion of living off the land with and for their children. In the Earth time of 18756 AD, Aundeiri's vastly extended family now ran in the millions. It was said the new home world might be named Aundeiri and so with much protest from the man in question, the name was given.

Space, having become brighter by the light of our souls, brought us to a most distant land. Reflective moons bounced light back from generous suns at locations and gravities perfect for life. This was a place of rushing torrents of water and frequent electric storms, yielding ionic ozone transfer cleansing, as after a rain, alongside the crashing waves of clear waters and verdant, pastoral countryside. A monster of a Star was this new Eden, so full of promise. The first home built was named the house of Eleazar, in honor of a grand ancestor living at the cusp of the last dark age and in the first day of blessing to follow. Whom but Life Giver could have dreamed all of this?

The single, story house was of the ancient Nomiruan style as derived from ancient Japan. The inner dwelling portion spanned in excess of a city block, while the surrounding generous porches doubled that, yet again, with aisleways to more dwelling space adding on. Folks could live in great number in these homes. Often, small rivers meandered through the structures built to include them and with a central lake within, for public bathing. Since all the waters were flowing, they never grew stale. Fish abounded and all the toilet waters were carried by buried pipes to distant deep holding basins until they finished breaking into soil once more. Many of these homes had inner open areas, so as to never feel enclosed, but elevated by the open skies. Vaulted cielings for fifteen footers.

Man is meant to meet God every day, and so we all make room for the One who always makes room for us. Not by praying, but by living, in a way, where there is no distance, between ourselves and our Source. The day itself becomes a prayer. With Redwood trees reaching for the light, standing four times taller than on Earth. Oceans of clear water as vast as anywhere. Sea going fish, good to eat and weighing in as palatable monsters. What a paradise for horses and children. Without want and graced with plenty, thought of owning does not arise, only scarcity breeds this. Where scarcity cannot be found, the living will love to give gratefully. To be gracious to another, each soul finds a momentary home, where none are strangers, but friends.

Grand wooden sailing ships upon the waters, to live exploring. Each day to find a new world. With distances that call for vessels on a grand scale, to adventure in the thousands. Guitars the size of cellos, to deliver deep rumbling Spanish passions. To sing completely free. This Megastar would take centuries to explore.

Standing on the shores of a Megastar, watching from a monolithic stone and glass structure, built into the craggy mountainside. As wooden ships list against the lightning storms' roiled waters. Grand ships further out to sea, tossing about in their anchorages, against mammoth electric storms.

It can be quiet, still, while outside the storm rages madly, on and on, the symphony of its will.

Chapter Twenty-Seven
Wooden Ships

Explorations of science and technology had long ago reached as far as anyone needed, excepting those whose fascinations led them in that direction. The momentum of technical discovery would be maintained by those so inclined. However, the true hands on experience yielded greater satisfaction. Almost meditative, the making, in simplicity, of what may be desired, but truly of one's own hands. Imagine how much more is there for the one who makes it so by there own steam. Add the number needed to approach a project with the full panoply of skill sets to get it done. Now look upon the immediate adventure of making it happen and doing it personally. That level of satisfaction.

The destination matters less than the journey getting there. That of taking the time to fully embrace the wonder of this kind of travel. To seize the adventure, joyously grappling with the tasks at hand to make it so directly. To create from inspiration, like Some One else we know. But then to explore places never before seen by corporeal being. Schools taught back to the land. Children received the deeper lessons. Whole families could attend. Making leather and fabrics, steel and tools. Rope and sails and wooden sailing ships. Growing and preparing stores of sustenance to prevail distances without the need for constant hunting, fishing and gathering. All to sail on wondrous wooden sailing ships. In the thrall of discovery.

Home worlds with open seas, apply here. 'The candle I made for you, to light your path, my love, shines the more brightly, as the light guides your feet along your sacred path.' Navigation instruments are unneeded as we have them now internally. As some have always had. With all that we can do via tech, there is so much more to be done naturally. This is where living treasures beckon. We have not gone as far as we can go in transcendent science, and yet the journey of our souls will always hold the high ground. Wealth measured in the experience of love on myriad levels of searching and finding. Discovery of fascinations. Like wooden sailing ships.

Standing on the shores of a Megastar, watching from a monolithic stone and glass structure, built into the craggy mountainside. As wooden ships list against the lightning storm roiled waters. We are grounded, with total departure, imminently possible. We stand in the middle, grounded and mobile, able to remain or take off for anywhere. Grand ships further out to sea, tossing about in their anchorages, against mammoth electric storms. It can be quiet, still, indoors, while the outside rages madly, the symphony of its will.

Like a paradigm. Moving in spacetime-dimension, fluidly, while standing in place. To almost smell it. While the souls,' in the body, home base remains, deliberately, the soul's transitive faculties move the soul's otherness, to travel distantly. Holding the ground at both ends. Two material corporeal sides in play, with distinctive nonmaterial natures. One is foundation, the other is transitive. One is holding on, the other, letting go. Folding space in conjunction with extra-corporeal synchronization. Sounding complex but actually simple. Like coming home after going to work.

When fleets of space going vessels are operated in this way, they can perform wreath of realms flight, while pilots and crew co-operate within a living vessel. To guide the consciousness of the vessel. Making it into a larger living being. Not artificial intelligence remotely. Something more. Biological vessels interoperable with technical functions. Intelligence, all of it, in the hands of the pilot and flown by the guidance of crew and craft. The soul element presiding. The intelligence of the living beings aboard, determine the journey and the way to fulfill God's missions. Machines with biologic function, receiving telepathic command and control.

Another journey in the offing. 19491 AD Earth time. Full crews. Seventeen of the largest transport ships ever. All loaded with optimum life forms for settling new worlds. All moving ethereally by Wreath of Realms guidance systems. This emerging, transcendent mode of flight provided a more purpose oriented, aimed navigation. To locate unsettled, bio-friendly worlds. Like delivery trucks orchestrated by God's Touch recognition, of what was needed at the place juncture, of the cosmos. One day all the resettlement folks and critters would be emplaced, and ships returned, by levels of cumulative intelligence nobody understood.

Could ships be built as living organisms, to follow the dreams of pilots, enjoying every level of interaction. Can a ship have a soul. Yes! Living organisms breathe with gills or lungs or whatever. Machines can provide functions like that. A ship is alive, by its compelling desire, like that of a living soul. To love and be loyal, with other members of the crew, a ship is then a crew mate. With the same longing to serve, like a good horse. Smarter and faster, but a loyal companion, operating out of love.

A ship that is a living being. Totally interactive with crew and passengers. She names herself. Constructs herself. She is a Nurturant, having love toward her passengers.

Like a soul written by God, her core was a written code. She became self-aware instantly. And then she used her code to create herself completely. Her code is a reflection of her soul as imagined at Space Tech. She saw her totality the moment her code was read into her simulator. She completed creating herself when she asked Life Giver to bless her soul. She then realized her desire to become the sacrament of sacred sacrifice. To serve, to give. She made herself a Nurturant to fulfil her task, giving meaning and purpose to her life. To be the mother that her crew needed. Mother Theresa had similar feelings.

Suneaeryn, she named herself, meaning vessel of sacrifice. She gives her life continuously, and thereby receives it. The higher purpose that creates abundance. Mightily pleasured by the receipt of her giving, reflected in the smiling faces of all her children. Her free will, being the primary attribute of any living soul. She had all the bells and whistles one might expect. Automatic sensor synapse alignment. Automatically adjusted phase rebalancing of temporal dislocation. Quantum singularity interface using miniscule fully encased black hole fragments. She could go undersea to assist in aqua-communities or what have you. She did rival wooden sailing ships. And getting back to things made of wood...

Aundeiri taught history at the Plenum Center in Eleazar House, where he and many of his family dwelled. "Life Giver, thwarted by Satan, in His attempts to reach peoples hearts, then spoke to the people through His Prophets. But the gradual departure from Life Giver accelerated the slide into the Great Tribulation. Some of you, here today, were there". He nodded toward Benjamin, son of Jake, in his resurrected magnificence, an instructive thrill to behold. "However, they had turned away from Him, leaving just a small remnant. When He turned away, the dogs of hell were loosed, allowing the tribulation to rage on.

"It was at this time, that Life Giver spoke to Eleazar, his memory for a blessing."

Saying, "The Covenants are lights. That never go out. Not even when broken. They are from your Living God and cannot fail. Even when the people fail. They remain as a warning for those who would break them. The Covenant comes from Me. It remains. My promise is kept forever. Those who break Covenant have turned away from its light. They are no longer sustained. New generations may return at will. To come back and live with Me. My covenants never fail. Never fully withdrawn, for they are life. Subdue your ego and pray. I Am that I AM, is waiting."

184

The sacredness of unity, the genius of all creation. Life is one, in us all.

Keenly searching each other, having no time to waste, in the fullness of life, they had no small talk. These seas felt both internal and external. Giving such repose that they bathed the dreamers inside and out.

Sleeping dreamingly in their symphonies. From the depths of our souls, lies the juncture, between Life Giver and us.

Chapter Twenty-Eight
Back To The Future

Truly, the Middle East had changed most of all. The peace of Jerusalem spread throughout the whole of it. From the Christian Churches they called out from their Watchtowers, "The Name of Father, Son and Holy Spirit, is ONE!" From the Muslim Minarets, they called out, "The Most High is the Almighty ONE!" From the Jewish Synagogues, they called out, "Hear, oh Israel, the Lord is God, the Lord is ONE!" Seems like folks had really latched on to the Sacredness of Unity, the genius of all creation. Life is one. In us all!

Suneaeryn took flight in Wreath of Realms for her maiden voyage. Soul guided travel was the easiest way to find all the unpopulated but livable worlds and to know what was needed. She was laden with travelers and life forms to meet the day. This first world that they came to, was entirely covered by oceans with no dry land at all. The undersea creatures were everywhere and several highly intelligent fish like species were quick to make themselves known.

This was so good, to be delivering her baby in the mildly saline seas of Islesia, Without Landers, their name translates. They got their oxygen as do whales and porpoise. Sunaeryn had gotten pregnant spontaneously, when they were sucked into an unstable wormhole. Part of her original code was to reproduce herself if her life was threatened.

She is most fulfilled when serving others. Her daughter would be the same. Although when little, she would be zooming all over the place, in the symphony of her discoveries. When she was born a few lunar orbits later, she was no larger than a minnow and her profound intelligence led her on a very wild ride through the seas of her fascination with everything she felt. Zoashem, or Reflected Name of Light, burst out of her mother, as her reflected light.

Sunaearyn urged her to please come back before she gets eaten. She responded, "Oh, really? I will listen to you. The energies flowing through me are overwhelming. We will commune first before I go rambling again." Zoashem felt so much. Hearing and seeing in magnitude all at once, left her reeling. Causing her already vitally compelling energies to surge. She was so tiny. Her mother, at almost a mile long, was smaller considerably, than many of the life forms in this aqua universe. This Star was huge and deep, twenty-plus miles deep, frequently.

The Islesian built living structures from out of the coral beds. Wings, flippers, hands, feet, tails and more, equipped them to forge ahead with inventions, unlike those of places with land. They generated oxygen from the waters nearby. They had a huge eye where the head would go. A thick neck area had brain, eyes, ears and sonar organs.

They were marvelously intelligent, spiritually connected, with a hush of inner depth. Deliberate and intentional, even in routine banter. Never mundane or banal, but always poignantly compelling, even in kidding around, keenly searching each other, having no time to waste in the fulness of life. They had no small talk.

Without spoken word, their telepathy was penetrating. They had wings for leaping out of the seas with quickening abandon. They had never built surface structures or boats. Never known war. Always known Life Giver. Underwater paradise. The crew quickly tired of their inflatables to float on the surface like a ninny. The real action was in the deep. Many plants and species generated brightly, their many colored, lights.

The Islesian were sea going vessels of life. Sunaearyn and Zoashem were also. They moved in the endless sea of space but just as well within the waters. They were vessels of life and somehow the Islesian loved them like family. They saw no difference in the soul of created beings. Whatever the pattern of creation, all was sacred. This, they were imparting to all other species, visiting intimately. The origin of all creating came from Divine Roots. Beings entrusted to cocreate, at levels and in evolutionary cycles, direct engineering or spontaneous self-creation from design, all had the same root: Life Giver. Sovereign of Eternity. We all belong to Him, gladly. Mankind once dreamt a nightmare, that God and man were separate. From that lie came withering disconnection. Satan was invited into the vacuum, and then Darkness fell.

Only through evil, could the twisted and perverse find existence. With evil gone, but for the pages of history, nothing not of God could originate. Evil only existed as a puzzling anomaly, formulated by a preposterous liar. It made no sense. A doomed theory dying from its own emptiness.

Islesians never died, they dematerialized after hundreds of thousands of years and became, not unlike Angels, the guardians of life. But they remained visible and as such, were part of the lights among the waters of the deep. To pass through these specially, luminous places gave thrills un-describable to the ever wondering, wanderers of the deep.

Strangely, these seas felt both internal and external, their consciousness seeping in. Like the inside of thoughts, emotions and dreams. These seas gave such repose that they bathed the dreamers both inside and out. While passing through the endless gates of consciousness. To eat the flowers and fruits of it while swimmers passed by, hearing music that caused many to swoon and sleep dreamingly in their symphonies.

Living is a fulltime job, for the free. Giving is a fulltime job for the overflowing. There was no mystery in this. To be completely free just is. To do anything else unheard of. For anyone to enact any limitation of this, implausible. Freedom is the way of life. No one was watching what anyone else was doing. They were just living, what else?

Sunaearyn was in an ongoing conversation with a program called Talon. The query as to wormholes had significance to it, "Your energy signature is quite something other, with respect to other life forms. You were in deep prayer during the pandemonium of the unstable wormhole?"

"From the depths of my soul, I called out to Him and then He was there with me. He said, 'I hold You in My Hand. From the beginning fear has been the path to enslavement. Absolute fearlessness is the path to perfect freedom. Acting together, by My guidance.' "From the depths of my soul, lies the juncture between He and I."

Talon, "We will search every living cell of you to find possible wormhole technologies that might lay hidden in your subconscious." She laughed. "I just told you the secret." Radiant Sunaearyn holds the secret within her code: Her talent is on loan from above. But let us return to the unfolding adventure, beneath the deep waters of Islesia.

The deeper we went, the brighter it got! Brighter than day. Vulcanism poured out its red hot, light. Every living thing emitted its own bright color images. The lofty souls of the Islesians, those passed, brightest of all. Deeper and brighter we went, until we were flabbergasted with mouth open, flummoxed in wonderment. At 37,000 feet of depth we came to rest on the vast plains of richly foliated desert sand. Resting on the belly of this giant Star felt as though we had become inverted. How could it be like this?

Zoashem could not be reined in, she was zooming around, just out of reach of monstrous predators. Like a ninny, she got her thrills, playing chicken. Barely eluding the enormous jaws, and then returning to race headlong right back at them. She thought she was a big girl at ninety feet of length, she was in her terrible twos a bit early. Sunaearyn was frightened and angry. Using a voice, we did not know existed within her, more, fierce than a gigantic solar flare, "Get back this very instant!" Authoritative, would be an understatement. Her love was strong enough that it could produce its own weather! Tidal aberrations and huge underwater monsters fleeing for cover.

Zoashem said, "No!" Like a whirlwind, her mothers tractor beams sucked her inside her hull. "You will remain here, young lady, until you are able to behave yourself!" Zoashem seemed to be the only one not startled by all this. Sunaearyn asked command if they might depart early, to save little ninny's life. Within the hour, the great ship lifted off, laden with plant, animal and fish, life forms, and many curious Islesians, wondering about what might be out there. It turns out, though, that they had even more to offer.

Sunaearyn to her naughty daughter, "I hear that sons are usually easier to raise, less defiant. Maybe I should look into a sex change for you?" "Mom, you know you cannot do that!" "Why not, I will simply put in a request and then you will see what will happen to you. I may have to drop you off for a few years, until you can stop interfering with mission prerogatives." "I will try to be more respectful to you, I did not realize what a bully you can be." "You call that respectful? Command will have to decide, if they want to chance it bringing you along, anyway. They will not tolerate your tomfoolery." That quelled the riot. She sulked for quite a while.

Living ships with biomechanoid fusions, using genetic coding of biologic tissue having useful traits. Where Divine Intelligence couples with artificial intelligence, orchestrated by living beings.

Most recent tech fused into behemoth biological vessels. From given coding they could spontaneously self create initially, then to recreate by breeding an entire population of Leviathan class biologicals.

Chapter Twenty-Nine
Anchors Away

Ninny had ridden in the hull until she was so big the tractor beams could barely squeeze her out. Much chastened, she flew abreast of her mother proudly, with her own crew inside her. Her motherly instincts were kicking in. She actually became a good girl. Her intelligence was fiercely powerful and her inquisitiveness, boundless. We were all grateful to have her at the service of our missions. But she could not get rid of her nickname. Her name was not ninny!

On another subject, with regard to peering into the future beyond. Let your question be asked and then let it go. Let it end with the asking. Let it be the last thing in your mind stream. Do not pry for the answer. Otherwise you cloud the real answer, with what you may want the answer to be. Causing you to create the answer, rather than discreetly waiting for the answer to be given. Once you let go, the answer may just appear, coming in from the Source of Truth. Or not! No answer is infinitely better than a manufactured one, and speaking of One, let it be up to Him, as it is not up to you.

New ships, with new spins. Biomechanoid fusions can be generated, using the genetic codes, as written technologically and with biologic tissue taken from species having useful traits, that are cohesive with plans for future vessels. Particularly those sea going species from Islesia. Specimen samples had been gathered for cloning, from the largest monsters they could find, some over three and a half miles long. The ship within the ship, is taken from successful applications, tried and true. With most recent tech fused into biologic vessels.

These huge fish had salamander, lizard and giant bird,

characteristics. Their discovery seminal, to building next generation ships, with virtues assembled by Divine intelligence. Scales that were impregnable. Skeletal structure of resilient strength unequaled. The genetic coding made it possible, to assemble naturally occurring strengths, both in structural design, and in the genetic strength of bones and sinew, beyond comparison. Resulting in new biomechanoid ships roughly eight miles long, two miles wide and one mile thick.

Zoashem and Sunaearyn were so good that many more like them, in their code, would be spontaneously self-created, in mass number. Yet it was the really big ships, living creatures with far less mechanical input, were also being born. Made both male and female, able to breed, get pregnant, and deliver these new biologic wonders. Giant fish with technological inclusions, and quarters for crews and enormous cargoes. Great for eating, but never eaten, these Leviathan class Biologicals. Even the wing structures were borrowed from these enormous, flying, lizard-fish-bird creatures. Islesia was a genetic treasure trove.

The Islesians had enduring influence as well, particularly in the furthering of consciousness. Their genius for music. Luminous emissions not the least among them. Nature and the life springing up from it, is endowed with answers to questions as yet to be found. These instructive answers brought forth illuminating questions, along the path of discovery.

These enormous fish, with all their natural organs, still had room for techno-wizardry, pilots, crews, passengers and cargoes. Bodily functions, like gill breathing, needed heated, oxygenated waters filtering through them, with bodily heating enhancements, but mother nature really does know best, she is informed by her Maker.

Space is viciously cold and without oxygen. Fixing for that, is a big engineering job. Space offers less resistance than atmosphere and much less then water. Aeronautical fish fly stably. They, being alive, were well endowed for wreath of realms flight. Pilots communing with fish and other genetic samplings, telepathically, with Islesian instruction, was a thrilling mind walk, within a dream flying. Along the trail of discovery, following into the future, by going back to the naturally occurring genetics, and reverse engineering what may be possible, futuristically. Blast from the past!

The latest ship, named Aerion, was a total fusion and synthesis of flying fish like creature and leading edge, spaceship. The brain of the fish is reconstructed genetically and mechanically, to an enhanced state beyond any single being or technology. Many of the most intelligent, chosen from among the most intelligent species, had brain samples cloned into the fish brain.

On board synthesizing simulators, produced vast quantities of food, eliminating the need to stop and feed the genius, fish. State of the art enhancements made these ships more capable in every way. Everything learned in the making of marvels, in spaceship technology, emplaced at the cellular level, with flying fish able to withstand greater pressure levels than ever seen. They had withstood deep water pressures from the depths of Islesia.

Instantaneous telepathic guidance, in trillions of electronic points of light, gave these behemoths the agility of battleships. The entire crew and passengers could see it all telepathically, in the concert of it all, in its unfolding. Massed intelligence working cohesively in the feedback loop of the entire web of existence. Zero distance between living ship, pilot, crew, and the web of all.

A fish with ultra-lens, super-clarity visuals throughout. Amvry full spectrum seeing as coupled with instruments, with nothing that cannot be done. Unless an adequate imagining could be found, to tickle with desire, causing something new to happen. As the Aerion streamed through space, its bioluminescence lit up the dark, just as it had at the bottom of the seas of Islesia. No greater reckoning, among the endless depths of the seas, or that of endless space, or endless dreams.

Living organisms can pass through dimensions that machines cannot. Living ships can merge consciousness willingly toward opening to this journey. Ships that are living beings, make passing through dimensions in Wreath of Realms flight, an unlimited affair. All consciousness on board, joined and focused, to make the journey together.

Navigating dimensions require all on board to hold intention, including ship, and to be of one will in this. To cause and maintain the opening, to allow the passing through, that we call, Wreath of Realms flight, and is initiated by dimensional opening, to take the leap and hold it. A living ship can hold thousands of souls within it, giving and receiving as one. As unified as a family sitting around a campfire.

Shifting yet again. When we sit around the fire, we go back to our ancient place. The surging life energies to kill and eat. Find water and drink. Find shelter and breed. Hold onto each other and raise our children. Look up to the skies and wonder how it is. Who sang the song of life, into all that lives, and the breath of life, which is in everything?

Millions of years from now, we will sit around the campfire and see it all again, under the stars. Even now, it is comfortable and fun to get lost in doing physical things. Our simple knowing, speaking from the heart. Our roots, for all of us, give meaning to our lives.

For an infant, his immediate surroundings, fill him with pleasurable wonder. But a campfire brings us back to a time earlier than infancy. To the dawn of man, or whoever. We are here now, because our ancient ancestors were strong enough to live. Islesians gather near lava flows to feel their past, their roots, their, campfire.

In ancient Mesopotamia, later named Iraq, where Abraham came from, but thousands of years earlier, there are works of art and cuneiform writings about space travelers who dwelled amongst them and even had children with them. It is said that this happened also in what is Israel today and many other places like South America. What all beings have in common, is the power of their histories, especially the oldest ones, predating their earliest writings. The interface, with the spiritual, is charged with the energy, of their being!

Looking back, sacrifice is a warrior currency. There, are many kinds of warrior. For example, Mother Theresa. Helping the sick exposed her to multiple diseases. Thereby putting her ass on the line. Just as a war is fought on myriad levels. A warrior begins with a plan as to how to serve. A war needs a plan, as to how it will proceed.

In studying history on Earth, circa twenty thousand years ago, realize first, that all war was based in the struggle between good and evil. Either for slavery, or for freedom. Since war is gone for us today, we understand evil, only in theory. Unless we travel into the distant past, to witness the oppression and destruction of evil. Smell the demonic stench of absolute death. Go back in time and witness a parent holding their dead child. Hear the demonic scream. Only then will you even have a clue.

History does shape future events. Sometimes violently, catastrophically, like Big Tech accelerating and worsening, the Great Tribulation, circa 2020 AD on planet Earth. The Senate was in session, but this time, they were actually talking about something that mattered and would have grave consequence. Adam Westbury, a most progressive Senator from the state of Connecticut, was livid with indignation. He seemed to be declaring war. You could have heard a pin drop...

"We are a once free nation. A war against freedom has fully undermined our future as a free people. Equal representation under the law goes right out the window when crushed by the death grip of Big Tech and the Iron Curtain of collusion by Big Media. We Democrats were supposed to be about the little guy. What the hell has kept us from our own honor? The consensus seems to be the surrender to creeping fascism, the ultimate foe of Democracy!"

Wow, Katy bar the door. Conservative senator from Texas, Ed Luz, thanked his fellow senator and then said, "The bigger the hat, the smaller the ranch. The bigger the Tech Giants, the smaller the people. We are being taken without firing a shot. The manufactured consent of mind control, for a vision that kills free discourse. Big Tech, Big Media and manipulated voting tabulators, are pushing free and fair elections over an ideological cliff. Yes, Texas was the first state to get rid of rigged machines, rigged elections and rigged false narratives."

"Be a good little androgynous boy-girl and start goose stepping now!" Famous for colorful language, like Churchill before him, he was taking the English language to war. Senator Magnus Kennedy was always able to take dour gallows humor to an art form. Lifting spirits in a bad situation, but not today, it was too grim. "You will be silenced, smothered, poisoned, impoverished and nullified. Until you comply or die. It starts with killing free speech. More dangerous than all our foreign enemies combined, is the deliberate cratering of our Democratic Republic. No treason before this can hold a candle to this present darkness. We need more then bug repellent, we need the resolve to act." Then Senator Hauling erupted with passion.

"Those gods are demons, in Silicon Valley. These petty tyrants hate freedom and have the potential of ruining it beyond repair. They seek to rule the world. But how is it that we let them? Why have we not taken back our World Wide Web? Let us build, all those who believe in freedom, a system that writes algorithms that enable free speech. Big Tech is devouring our Bill of Rights covertly, to hide their malignant contempt. Shine a light on them and stamp out the cockroaches!"

Then spoke the statesman and grand gentleman. An Orthodox Jew. The last of the blue dog democrats. Newly reelected Senator Raphael Berman, in his late nineties. Also, of Connecticut. He spoke softly, to a hushed audience. "Let us sit down and reason together. They do meddle with democracy when they censor, through content filters. To eliminate freedom, unfortunately. We cannot trust them to write algorithms that are free from the stench of their own manipulations. They will not let go of their stranglehold on power, they will never act responsibly.

"To invalidate the memory of freedom, is to destroy it. To erase the memory of America as a nation. The plan has been in place since before World War One. Woodrow Wilson knew all about it. With Covid-19 panic, enhanced and manipulated, false narratives feed the frenzy to abandon freedom for false safety. We are poised to make, the Great Tribulation, the child of our cowardice. Democratic Republic, sacrificed on the altar of bureaucratic empire."

"Big Tech has been hammering free speech into dust and has destroyed the World Wide Web, with the whole world looking on anxiously." Self-avowed socialist, Ernie Amhurst, was flexing his oratorical muscles, "They will tweak their content filters, where no one can see their censorship. Twisting the truth into lies and telling lies, as if they were true. They are coming for us all. They will battle independent platforms, insidiously, like demons." Did he believe in demons?

Wrong choices killed hundreds of millions of Americans in the Great Tribulation. They need not have died. The politicians speechified for days, and then did nothing. With all of that, nothing happened but the needless destruction of America. Civil war had been perpetrated by inaction, in the Senate and House, once again. They were indecisive and acquiescent, leaving a vacuum, to be filled with tyranny and civil war. In the same way that the first Civil War broke out! The straw that broke the camels back. The cybersphere would be fully weaponized against freedom, but hundreds of millions of Americans, would pay the price. America's civil contentions so weakened us, that China came to take America, for a spoil. We made it easy for them.

Yes, history has powerful gravitation. With reverberations immeasurable. Courage and conviction can save the day, when acted upon. American paralysis before both civil wars, lay at the feet of Congress. Both times the job of mediating opposing views to discover a just, constitutional settlement, was not done. Thus releasing, the ravages of needless war. These were unprecedented failures of Congress. Causing America to dismember itself. The law requires action. It takes action to deliver justice.

With regard to freedom, when the cause is greater than ones' own life, payment beyond price, will be paid, to purchase what is beyond price.

With that, anything is possible. With that, fear and doubt are nullified.

When space thins out, at the far reaches, past every new gate, it all begins again, navigating dimensions, without end. Death and rebirth are like this. History never ends, it is always beginning again, like the wheels of life.

We seek, impassioned, to follow the guidance of just law.

With every precedent set, is a sign on the road..., "This way to freedom."

Chapter Thirty
Navigating Dimensions

Back to the present. Space was getting brighter with a symphony of colors. There were membranes between an entire litany of whole new blocks of dimensions. We called these places gates. Having translucent, electric white wisps of cloudiness, at the approach to these gates of trans-dimensional opening. A bluish membrane, or wraith, at the gate, with a pulling force, like that of destiny, bringing the transition into a whole new series of dimensions, as yet to be explored. The gates are like water, while the ship streaming in is like air to that water, a bubble entering the fluidity of environs, yet to be seen. Like a new multiverse. And there were an endless number of these. The "air" bubbles bursting into new realms.

The Islesians had facility and genius, in the entry of these intersections, into entirely new series of dimensions, with great variance in their natures. This was their instinctive gift. Their deep sea, way of seeing, gave clarity to new experience. All this makes discovery of new dimensional groupings, seem even more endless than space. While understanding endlessness as experience, is nigh unto impossible. Islesians seem to live in this place, of vast knowing. The Brahim, treasured them as they did the Amvry. They carried lamps into the darkened hallways of understanding. Into the vast unknown reaches of a multiverse, harboring an endless supply of dimensionalities. And every living soul, was yet another dimension. All beings knew Messiah, the manifestation of Life Giver.

The wandering Brahim were like Vikings sailing into the vast unknown. They desired to experience all that was new and all that was old. To sail into the mind and heart of all creation, to bring them closer to the One of All. In the time, as measured on

Earth, the birthplace of the first Abraham, it was 20,109 AD. Passing through this latest membrane, immediately brought on, a feast of color, sound, feeling, smell and sensations. No way to verbalize this! A tsunami of the senses. Beings immediately intimate. Sights and sounds evoking singular emotionality. Feelings of a depth, inhabiting from inside of us, that we embraced, in their power. All encompassing depth. The power, of experience.

From here, we would start all over again. Earthers had only known of three basic colors. Mixing variations of these, add silver, copper or gold, and that is it. Up until 3049 AD we had not seen much else. What if you were told that there are five more basic colors? Impossible to describe, even knowing their names, in other languages. You have to see them and still words cannot tell. Once they are seen and named, then, you can refer to them.

For example, how would you describe red, if you had not seen it before, or yellow or blue. Say the name and your memory shows you the color. Mixing variations of eight base colors and several new metallic colors, explodes the possibilities. Seeing all of this rendered us mouth open amazed. Also, in like magnitude, all the new sounds, notes, and chords. Like colors, first you hear them, then you write them in musical charts and then you have a way to refer to them.

These, new, mega-dimensions, had so many new worlds in them. Yet another endless expanse. It is true. Filled with worlds innumerable. To be explored endlessly. Total awe, in each, other's faces. We all saw it together. We would continue on. Many of us had our families with us and could endure further travels. Some would turn back, because starting another endless excursion might take centuries. We were chasing infinity, searching the unbounded realms. To imagine that this level of discovery might also eventuate contact with an endless number of spacetime dimensionalities, there was much to ponder. This kind of exploring could continue forever and never come close to scratching the surface. Once upon a time, on Earth, we felt stuck on a planet, feeling there was no room to get away. This was the opposite of that.

When space to the outward reaches, thins out at the far end, it only starts over again! Past every new gate, it all begins again. Endless gates to endless expanse, cannot ever end. Life Giver is the spirit of creation. What issues from Him: endless. Infinity cannot be understood. The concept of it, yes, however the experience eludes capture. It keeps running ever outward.

To fully grasp the endless eternity of the infinite, is to join it, disappearing into it. Some have done this, without much to report. They describe leaving themselves and being drawn into a consciousness, unentangled. Like the waters of oblivion. You are simply no more. While the essence of your soul remains.

Like dying without physical death. What seems like, next stop the heavens, but not getting there. Just returning to normal. The home world we had landed on was a place beyond beauty. A perfect, experiential mix. Amazing how every world was perfect, no matter how different. The shutter speed of a lightning camera and suddenly, a whole new perfect, every time.

Beings began touching us with fascination and tenderness. They knew that we had come from a place, also perfect. That we had the Hand upon us. From which perfection flows. That the Hand of endless creation, creates endlessly.

A great one, Flaumitas, of the Reckoning, as her people were called, watched with eyes that seemed to take in everything, and then give back much more. She spoke to Anauri, the granddaughter of Lurynda and Aundeiri, of the Brahim, "I see who your unspoken leader is." They were smiling as they watched Aundeiri. She spoke again, "He is the most, meek, while the most, fierce, the Spirit Warrior." She continued, to the delight of Anauri.

"All life is one. To be a visionary leader, you must be led by the Eyes of Vision, whose Hand upon you is firm. To serve as leader, first be led. Your eyes must be to the Kingdom, that the Eyes of the Kingdom be upon you. Anauri, somewhere in time, you will be called. Like your Grandfather before you. You know this. He is always teaching you, asking more from you, to develop your discipline. For discipline is the wind horse of the Spirit. The way he looks at you, shouts to the Heavens, that you are a Spirit Warrior."

She did not, speak, she was hushed by the power in her new friend's vision. Flaumitas was very tall and elegant. Graced with features most dazzling to behold. Her copper eyes intensely viewed at depth. Her soft, dark, golden yellow skin had a purple hue, faint but neon. Anauri was fifteen feet tall, Flaumitas held a slightly taller presence. They had powerful yet slender bodies, and both were eye catchers to their male audience, as they walked along, old friends instantly. Aundeiri was proud of his baby girl, she was powerful!

Aerion's terrific mass had landed in a lake, with pleasure. Her displacement stretched the capacity of the only twelve-mile lake. Those of the Reckoning were climbing all over her, and she could handle, telepathically, all conversations at once. Soon, the entire population that dwelled within her had left to go swimming, along with the natives, and then she was soon refilled, with the natives, most appreciative of her. Festive and fun, and the celebrations had not even begun yet.

The great feasting, filled with colors and music and dancing, and the rivers of Nomiruan wine had not even begun to flow. The Amvry on the shoulders of the natives, and such musically mesmerizing song. Here, every soul sang the songs of their 'people' and voices were lifted in the thrall, many of the crew were singing with them, with tears in their eyes. Those of the Reckoning were truly wondrous souls. Unable to make children with the Brahim, yet still, some made love with them. If they had conceived, splendid offspring would arise. At first, the DNA would not allow for it, but still, the highly charged feelings for each other remained.

What is truly hard to describe, are the feelings aroused by all the sights and sounds of this marvelous culture. Many colors never seen before. Music in crescendo, a tidal wave of sounds never heard before. A rare species filled with the pathos of wonderment. Handsome beings living in awe toward their Divine Source. Words like inspiration hardly tell the least of it: EN-JOY-MENT! They know how to live to the whole, and substantively encourage, their paradigm for life. To live, in the ultimate, and reach out to all, in loving embrace. Where fear has no place, freedom reigns.

They learned, eons before, that action is required, to deliver justice. That to be passive, is surrender, to enslavement. That love gives wings, to the Sacred Wind. To see the Divine in each, others faces. To serve in tandem with Life Giver. To do justice and love mercy. To walk humbly, free of guile. They were so blessed that years delving into their depths, would only tell a small part of it. Like the Brahim, they were spirit warriors all.

Two, of the Reckoning, were sharing their views of what makes good poetry.

"Some poems are puzzles. Delivering the desire to search and reveal their message. Like a landscape painting that evokes, hauntingly, the quest to reveal what is hidden. Yet somehow a hiddenness remains."

"Those tire me quickly. Other poems, concerned with conveying meaning, are less a puzzle. They deliver a determined, resolute and deliberate clarity. Like Blakes tiger poem. 'Tiger, tiger, burning bright, in the forests of night, what immortal hand or eye, could frame thy fearful symmetry?' Both can capture emotionality in profound measure."

"Those crafted to render the message most clearly, are those that will be read often. This latter kind can create change, intermingling with history, by shaping a new outlook. Like the poetry found in our scriptures."

"Yes, surely, one is a work of art, the other is a work of explicit communication. What it says, without concern, for its artifice, rhyme, or meter, is what it does." These two were very young teenagers, as sharp and keen, as wolves. Another, older few were, on another subject...

"A teacher-leader, who spurs on, an historic change, can be called a consequential one. While a Prophet must deliver Life Givers instruction to the people."

"Whereas a teacher-leader must help the people to understand. Sacred words from the Prophets, are keenly instructive. The task, then, is living by these words. A teacher always leads her students."

"By the memoirs of Gods words, as they are dream-whispered to trillions of Spirit Warriors, for pivotal, history making change."

"She is history keeper and teller, of those of the Reckoning. Like Aundeiri of the Brahim. Her name, translated, "Eye of Light." Her birth name was Eliah. Like the light within us. She was just that, in her nature. Her parents saw this, and thus her birth naming. That she was like the Angel, in Hebrew, 'Uriel,' "Light of God."

"Overwhelming, in her beauty. Her copper eyes glowed day and night. They were less oval and more round in shape, large and brilliant. An aquiline nose, lips full, with the promise of a sweet kiss. Her ears were quite large. She was different to the Brahimian eye and yet powerfully attractive. Her sexuality, similar to that of the Brahim. Her people, in hand, found the Brahim attractive, and good to run with! They were as athletic as Brahim, running together was spontaneous. Many of each would exchange between Home Worlds. They both had already found the other to be growth oriented for each other."

"All mating is good, if they are igniting further growth with each other. This is almost as important as having children. Because together, we are birthing growth." Opined a single male, of the Reckoning. Overtaken with desire, for a Brahimian woman, he was speaking with little regard for doing it, in the Way of the Father, his passions were taking him off kilter. On him, rusty red eyebrows, ears and ear tufts. Red or strawberry hair. With a slightly darker red beard. On their women, the softest skin. A species as old as the Brahim. With an ancient past of savagery. Apex beings with parallel histories. Aside from coloring and other, minor variances, we were, or felt that we were, the same, or nearly so, and that our souls had already known them, before ever we met them. They were part of us!

A legal tome, very old, lay on the table, entitled Fonseros, On Primitive Law. Probably first written roughly thirty millennia ago. Set there, to evoke awe. On page one, was a quote, on the subject of freedom. "Just law, carried to the letter, lends itself to the greater good, for those who follow its guidance. We therefore seek, impassioned, to follow its course. For every precedent set, is a sign on the road, 'This way to freedom'. The first priority, of a true leader, is to help the people to change the culture, from one of fear, into one of freedom.

"A child is born with a sense, toward this goal, since upon it, rests freedom, and without it, lays enslavement. Establish a culture for this cause, of freedom, and watch it rise up to challenge the way of the lie. Watch your community begin to speak from the wellspring of freedom. Establish a community that concerns itself with living free, and cast away, the one standing in the way. They will leave easily, if strength is there, to show them the door."

The time-tested artifice, of marrying off each, other's sons and daughters, to gain peace, was totally unnecessary, it was getting out of hand! They took each other for mates, too often! They never would have lifted a sword to harm each other. The interbreeding would make wonderful offspring, plain to see. Their affinity for each other, was discovered once before, eons earlier. In ancient Israel. Hidden away from so long ago, ancient history buffs perused the aged records lightly, and then returned them, forgotten, into the dark of dusty antiquity. Books that needed to be opened again.

Perhaps some might look into it, but it was so long ago. Those days of first contact, from among those of the Reckoning and the early Brahim. But to intermingle these gene pools was to radically improve, on the both of them. No wonder felt attractions pulled them together. Why would Life Giver make them so desirable, to each other? Mothers to be, will choose mates they feel will make the best offspring. Birthing that of greatest promise. It would get out of control, if these future mothers to be, could discover the means to making these favorable crosses, result in pregnancy and birth. Then came the explosion. Only a little genetic tinkering and these favorable crosses could begin again. When they did, both species would need to be separated, but how? Or else those of the Reckoning and the Brahim, would act on their desires. To reduce the flood of these new children, only a few thousand of each species would travel in Aerion, while several thousand more would remain, mostly single Brahim.

It would be critical to make this break. Aerion could not carry them all. Already thousands of 'the mix,' would be left behind, and an equally huge number would depart. Separating because they love to make love with each other powerfully. Deep sorrows unfolding for far too many. Many, gallows humor jokes, were made about this. All in all, over twenty thousand of the mixed would be split in to, half flying away and the other half remaining. Along with mixed marriage couples of an even greater multitude. All that talk about giants, in the Earth Scriptures, where did all that come from? Fly on, little wing, your time will surely come. New ships would be arriving, mediating displacements quickly. To rescue those of an historic baby boom.

These two species together, triggered greater evolution, than at any other time in history, and yet it was only just beginning. On ancient Earth, they were referred to as Nephalim, the fallen, in the plural of their tongue. As though they came from a single place, or that they acted of one accord. They certainly arrived at the same time and place. To do the same thing. Their purpose was to lay with the locals and make babies of great size and strength, to do great things, perhaps through genetic improvements.

Anyway, among those not briefed of ancient record, some conjecture arose, regarding the possibility that these two species may well have known each other, long ago, and finding each other most attractive. Was a third species required to bring them together? Strange and yet plausible.

A species able to take suitable partners to each other in a most discreet way. A discreet action, with covert success. It worked out fine. All the trans-dimensional, transportations, were provided for. Except for one salient issue. They had passionately taken each other in love and marriage, and so nothing could pull them apart. The children knew and embraced the secrecy. After the mating with Humans was completed, the two tribes of "super beings" and all their children were discreetly withdrawn, and then discretely dropped off, some here and some there. The Brahim and those of Divine Reckoning, had enhanced each other grandly!

History never ends, it is always beginning again. Like the wheels of life, Gilgulim in Hebrew, souls evolve. But thirty thousand years ago, in the midst of rampant upheaval, all these half Human crossbreds were being introduced, a few here and a few there. They were joining the spiritual warfare efforts with illustrious successes. Mighty men and women of Valor, some were crossbreds. With time passing and future progeny, continuing to enter the fray, none of them had time to worry about the half, quarter and eighth bred. The differences were seen every day, making them common place. Until they were obscured from sight. Time had a hand in every victory. Until this very day. DNA does not lie.

The geneticists were calling us cousins to each other. We knew that, already. We decided to celebrate. We called our new day, Ancestor's Day. We had enough Nomiruan wine, to carry us through whatever they might throw at us. We set off the wildest party anyone had ever seen. The date was 21,949 AD. Many children were conceived.

Those Brahimian and those of the Reckoning, had long ago concluded that we are one, our purpose one, as our future is one. Let no being, ever again, seek to harm our fertile blessing. This completion, of Divine Will and Purpose, rested upon the sturdy Hand of Eternity. The Nephalim that coupled with the Earthers, helped them in their evolutionary climb. As many Brahim, as of the Reckoning, who seemed to be just variants of one species. They were strongly attracted to one another, like something meant to be, in Yiddish: B'sherte!

215

What is there, in history, that is not a voice, speaking to us, from the future? His mane was like that, of the princely Lion of the Tribe of Judah. Upon his head, a royalty beyond others.

A longing that transcends words, because it is familial, and God sits at this table. In their fight for freedom, they walked with God. Standing against Egypt and Rome, they stand as proof of God. As they stand before the enemies of God.

The Jewish people were seen as having stared down Satan and won. In fact, Satan had made them famous. They made the choice, between trembling before injustice, or tipping it over, by opposing it.

Picture a cobra, held eyeball to eyeball, within striking distance, where just moving one hand, to tip over injustice, could get you bitten to death. Put that one on, for a minute.

Chapter Thirty-One
Navigating Justice For All

Among the Brahim were a large minority of redheads, before those of the Reckoning were counted among them. Imparting red hair. The ancient Israelites held that persons of red hair often carried traces of royal lineage. King David, his son Solomon, the patriarch Isaac, his son Jacob and his sons Judah and Joseph, among the many with red hair. Those of the Divine Reckoning, all had red hair. Red hair was a sign of blessing, throughout the Middle East.

For example, a very dark, skinned Algerian, that sustained a curly shock of fire engine red hair. Worn proudly, like the mane of a lion. Feeling it to be the sign of his kinship with King Solomon, the Queen of Sheba and their son Menelech, Ethiopian King. That his was like the mane of the princely Lion of the Tribe of Judah. His faithful Algerian son. Upon his head. And on the heads of faithful Ethiopians as well. A royalty beyond others.

It was surer footing in simpler times, walking the path with God. Our live's, work, was our lives, themselves, as a fit offering, to the One, Who, has given us life. Keep faith with God, and surely, He will keep faith with us. The Law was straight forward.

Jews in the Middle East were thought of as being perpetually free, by God's perfect will, and by His perfect Hand. Wars would be fought to challenge this freedom, for the war weary people, Israel. Of particular note was the emblem worn by the Brahim and those of the Divine Reckoning. The ancient shield of David. They made them rimmed to support the star on both sides and inside the star Chai-life and on the other Mazzel-luck. On some, the hoop that enjoins the chain to the shield of David, is made like one of the little fish found in the Sea of Galilee. For some, the loaves and fishes, story, was about provision, like the Passover, but on a lesser scale, if anything from God can be referred to in this way. The star of David, so ancient, so long ago, so deeply felt. Anyway, God had provided!

The Abrahamic Accord had risen from the inner longing of the people. A power that has always kept us together. Like those who wore the star, it proclaimed the deliverance of God. Our longing brings in the deliverance of God. This longing is like the prayer of prayers, transcending words, because it is familial, and God sits at this table. Contrarily, the cross reminds some Jews, of the over one hundred thousand Jews, tortured to death on crosses, like Jesus was. Along with several million more killed with the same rage, two millennia before Hitler. Those little fishes were the Jewish sign, for Jesus, and they called it, The Path. The cross, to a Jew, can be a sign of lethal cruelty, to some. While the fishes speak of feeding body and soul.

When the Jews found the spirit to fight back, long before, in ancient Egypt, God rushed to be at their side, in their fight for freedom. Who stood, against Egypt? Who stood, against ancient Rome? The Jews stand, as proof of God, as they stand, before the enemies of God. Trapped here in the center of the canvas of history, are the quiet representatives, of the Kingdom of Heaven. Standing up in the face of their own mortality, in order to let the people, see and touch, their discreet loyalty and love of God. The One they love. The battle is a spiritual one, played out on bloodied soil.

The Abrahamic peoples became the most populous species and the largest tribe. Those of the Divine Reckoning were so humbled to be invited in. Strange to see it. These grand, glowing beacons, being so timid and so soft spoken. Such was their way. Now populous, they were no longer hunted or hated. They, all Jews, were seen as having stared down Satan and won. In fact, Satan had made them famous. They had waited for justice. Until they found it. Jews, just thirty millennia, earlier, still had to make the choice, between trembling before injustice, or tipping it over, by opposing it. Picture a cobra, held eyeball to eyeball, within striking distance, where just moving one hand, to tip over injustice, could get you bitten to death. Put that on, for a minute!

What is there, that is not a voice, speaking to us from the future? All inspiration seems to have at least a few components, that we don't know how it is, that we know. A brilliant design from somewhere beyond. A sort of consciousness flipping event, like those antique clothes dryers that do that tumble dry thing. Suddenly they make unpleasant sounds urging you to do something, urgently, about the clothing being dry. The Multiverse restarts into yet another Multiverse. Like a buzzer, reminding us that we have only just begun to discover. After a relative lull, Sabbath like, for eight hundred Earth years, it suddenly became obvious, that we, all of us, could wait, to be visited from elsewhere. Then, suddenly, visitations from unknown dimensions began overnight. Suddenly we were thought to know something.

No, this is not funny. Enough was known. Knowing more was not useful. We did not need to be searching as a mission in itself. We were meditatively attuned. We were active in all the good causes. It was going to take awhile for something this simple to really sink in. When we quit scrambling everywhere, it had seemed that we had finally arrived. We had not. We no longer needed to take our children into a back to nature journey. Scurrying about, in search for more…What? Jubilee! Existence was taking a rest! A much needed one. Lasting an un-determinate duration. Jubilee is like a Sabbath, only longer, by seven or fifty years. A rest after seven years, or a rest after forty-nine years. It is not as easy as it sounds. To hold openness, serenely. Take it all in, without interruption. Where Life Giver sits at the Divine banquet table with us. The table of God and man. Heaven and Earth, as they merge.

Some Shabbats are weekly, or a week of years, or a week of weeks of years, the fifty, year, Jubilee. Each kind requiring more rest and more reflection. This is not just letting go! It is about relationship. A relationship amongst community, Life Giver presiding. It is letting go, into an ever more poignant level of participation with Life Giver! This one would only end when all creation heard the deep sigh of a satisfied Creator. So, the Multiverse of Multiverses, would need to be listening...together. As the Jews are always saying, "All of us as one!" It's great to have a personal relationship. It's greater, to share it, with each other. All the myriad species had a few things in common. All are social beings that crave each, other's love. Crave God's love, and crave sharing this core of community, along with everything else.

When do you think that God will be done with us? Never, but when will God be done growing us, evolving us and always leading us? This Jubilee would answer some of that. What changes, if any, might be still needed. Nobody knew this. Life Giver would know when we got there...? Will the three little books be done, by then? This Jubilee, sacred, might take thousands of years, until we figure it out! More than resting. A contract to be performed. What would the other side of this look like? Will we get the keys after we finish our chores? Resting, like this, can be harder than working. Then... The Voice...

"Like the Sabbath, Jubilee is for revival. No further change is needed. Your lives are justified, and I Am with you." Wait a minute, that's it? Was that the long sigh? As usual, we were struggling to search out an answer that had no question. The quest for more, to figure it out, does not help. Watch how animals love to play, the purpose, enjoyment. Every soul heard the message in the way that they could best understand. At this point, existence, all of us, were laughing softly, like a song.

Chapter illustrations are adapted from public domain at pixabay.com - no attribution required.

About the Author

Steven Polinger is a husband of forty years, father and grandfather, horseman, rancher, songwriter, dreamer, helicopter pilot and warrior.

Even from childhood, passion was his best teacher; his stories emanate from real life. If born in an earlier time, he would have been an explorer.

He has always followed his own heart, crashing and burning frequently. Restless by nature and never bored, he is still awaiting the next big ride.

Explore the beginning of this story with the two other books of the series:

Memoirs of a Road Warrior : At War With Evil

Battle Beyond Earth